Memorial

Ferdinando Camon

MEMORIAL

Translated by David Calicchio

THE MARLBORO PRESS
MARLBORO, VERMONT

Originally published in Italian as
UN ALTARE PER LA MADRE

Copyright © Aldo Garzanti Editore, 1978

Library of Congress Cataloging in Publication Data

Camon, Ferdinando, 1935-
  Memorial

  Translation of: Un altare per la madre.
  I. Title
PQ4863.A392A813   1983   853'.914   83-60549

ISBN 0-910395-07-1

First printing 1983
Second printing 1991

The publication of the present volume has been made possible
in part by a grant from the National Endowment for the Arts.

MEMORIAL

1

In front of the church a small crowd had formed, children, women and men of all ages, who little by little regrouped according to family relationship, or at random: a word said by one person had only to be replied to by another, and the two would keep each other company. I ended up by myself and the last.

Some of the boys lifted the coffin to their shoulders and started off across the countryside, the others fell in behind, single file.

The narrow dusty path of sandy earth ran between stretches of wheat infested with poppies: wherever you looked there was more red than yellow, and there was a strong smell of green grass fermenting in the sun. Larks circled overhead, not many, and only a few were singing; the others wanted to land but were disturbed by the presence of humans. The men having passed, they waited yet a bit, then dropped down like stones, but without the thud of impact, for when only a foot or two from the ground, they opened their wings, beat them twice, rapidly, just enough to save themselves; then trotted off, gliding their necks between the stalks of wheat.

The coffin swayed on ahead.

I thought of my mother, and it seemed right that the coffin sway. My mother's gait had never been even, she was always pretty tired; she spoke little while she was working, would stop every so often to go and sit down without a word in the shade, under the vines, bowing her head.

Huddled like that, she prayed in silence. Now and then she would moisten her lips with her tongue, then wipe her forehead and her cheeks and her mouth with a handkerchief that was never an actual handkerchief: it could be a little sack that salt comes in, empty now and just washed, or the always preserved swaddling from her last child, or a clean rag taken from a drawer. She never thew anything away. She believed that tightly wrapping the legs of newborn babies in swaddling cloths would straighten them out. Before getting up from table, she would glance about to see whether there were not a few scraps left over and to prevent them from being thrown out; she would drink whatever remained in each glass, put the leftover soup in the cupboard, away from the flies.

A corner of the cupboard was always taken up with leftovers put there by her; when one of the children was hungry, she would open the door and with a smile show those leftovers, dried up and hard. They looked like ancient stones in the showcase of a museum.

She economized on everything. She would retrieve the coins swallowed by her children. In the country children used to play in the sand with small coins. In order to have their hands free, they put the money in their mouths (their pockets always had holes) and sometimes a child would swallow one: he'd feel it slip past under his tonsils, big as a bite too big to swallow, his eyes would bulge, he'd grow pale. The coin would struggle, turn, and slowly go down, scraping like a piston in a cylinder. The child would stop playing, would be declared the loser, and would run off to look for his mother, in the fields, in the street, in the house, wherever she might be. From the moment he found her he was under day and night surveillance—not because he was thought to be sick, but to recover the coin. There would be an anxious wait until he felt the need, an iron pot would be kept at hand. When the need occurred, he would squat over the pot and his mother would stand stiffly beside him, like a sentinel. The coin, coming out, would land upon the bottom with a metallic sound, copper striking iron. The child would be the first aware of it and would be off immediately, without even finishing what he was doing, pulling his pants up as he ran. His much gratified mother would pick up the pot and, her eye on the gleaming coin, would go to the pump and rescue it, separating it from the rest under the jets of water, as gold prospectors do. Coins were worth more than their face value. Whatever you bought you paid for in kind, through barter, and people never got their hands on any money, except, sometimes, those reddish copper coins, that were held on to like a hostage, kept under constant guard so that he won't escape. Our world had nothing to do with the rest of the world. It functioned on its own, and it was immortal. Even our mother, we had always looked upon her as something immortal, at least as immortal as the world. Because when we were born, she was already part of the world, the world without her was not conceivable.

Now my mother was dead, but that was not possible.

Some, one after the other, placed a hand upon her coffin, as if to touch her hand or shoulder: we are all here with you, do not be afraid.

The coffin weaves ahead along the path, floating over the fields of wheat.

The bearers halt every so often in the shade and the

file also moves off the path. Then we, the family, are able to find places around the coffin and put a hand upon it. I love the coffin, the wood it is made of. The flowers, leaf by leaf, petal by petal. Everything. I am not afraid of death anymore. This reconciles me with life. I think of something that I forget at once. Thinking of it again, I believe that if I were to relive this situation, I would experience the same thoughts again, but I am unable now to say what ones.

At last we reach the cemetery and enter the lane flanked by two lines of cypresses. Framing the entrance gate is an arch of stuccoed brick, with a Latin inscription painted in red. I don't think anyone in the village knows what it means apart from my father, who has asked the priest.

My father always tries to find out everything. He picks up all the scraps of paper he finds lying on the roads and brings them home. If they are wet he dries them near the fire, then flattens them out with the palm of his hand and reads them one by one. They all interest him, bits of newspapers, discarded letters, shopping lists and figures. From two words he is able to reconstruct a news despatch, from an illustration he can imagine the plot of a film, from a shopping list he can tell who may have done the buying. Certain families buy only bread but as they are ashamed of their poverty, they place the bread on dishes, so that it will be thought that even on workdays, and not just on Sundays, they eat soup or meat or greens.

One time my father found a bit of newspaper showing two people, a man and a woman. The man was standing with his back to a wall, staring at the reader with eyes popping out of his head, shirt sleeves rolled up, head shaven like Yul Brynner; and on his right was a young woman in tears, hands clasped in front of her. Friends sometimes dropped by to see us after supper. That night they discussed who those two people might be. As always, the most trenchant opinion prevailed: a little old man, wrinkled, scabby, tough, who had fought the war in an armored division and repeated all the time that a tank driver jumps when he is killed, pointed his finger and said, "Il duce." He had recognized him. Everybody looked. It must have been il duce at the moment of his execution, together with Claretta Petacci. Claretta, everyone knew her: she was the one whose face was engraved on coins, with the towers on her head. Attention enjoined silence, and silence gave rise to compassion for the two who were shot. Someone observed that the Americans would not have killed such a man. My father showed the picture to my mother because everything that came into the house and had any importance was to be shared. My mother looked at it with an expression of sadness, and shook her head disapprovingly.

Shooting a man was something she did not accept, even if he were the world's greatest criminal. To kill was for her the sin of sins. Once my father took us to the movies to see *The Sign of the Cross*. We sat well to the back, far from the screen which may be dangerous, you never know. My mother didn't understand how they got from one scene to the next: you saw Rome burning, then Nero singing with his lyre in his hand, but between one scene and another the separation wasn't sharp, you continued for a while to see the flames on top of Nero himself and my mother asked if he wasn't burning. My father did not answer, just shook his head. When the Apostle appeared, circling through the quarters of Rome, dominating them with his slow gaze, my father, who had already seen the film many times, urged us to pay particular attention to how he made the sign of the cross. The Apostle did indeed make it in an odd way, tracing in the dirt with the point of his staff first one right angle, then another, almost meeting at the top, like this: ⌐ ∟ . My mother tossed her head, that seemed to her a useless innovation. Then when they began to show the torturing of the Christians, I had the impression—but perhaps that impression only comes to me now—that my mother began to pray, there in the moviehouse. It was the one film she ever saw. The moviehouse remained for her a place where torturing was done.

We passed under the arch and entered the cemetery. The priest delivered a short speech, in a very quiet voice, talking with the dead one and with the Lord. Everyone had the impression that my mother

13

and the Lord were together, and that this was right. We, the family members, went up to the coffin one by one and we kissed it. The wood smelled very warm, as if human. Then the coffin was carried to the grave and lowered until it struck the bottom. Each one threw in a handful of dirt, then the earth shoveled in covered it over. There was as yet no vase of flowers, or lamp, or name. My youngest sister had a bunch of flowers and was looking for a way to arrange them. She planted them in the newly turned earth, as if they had roots, placing them in the shape of a cross. I walked out of the cemetery in a daze, I wasn't able to bear any more. I sat down in the grass at the edge of the road. At that same moment a flock of sheep was going past. The anguish inside me melted away as I looked at those animals with such human faces. As they moved along their heads went up and down as though to say yes to life every step of the way, and seen as a group, from behind, they formed a bobbing yellow froth. Bringing up the rear, several yards behind, was a wobbly lamb. I watched it as if something sad was about to happen to it. The sheepdog trotted up to it, took it delicately by the fleece, without hurting it, and pulled it up level with the group, putting it down almost directly in front of me. The lamb stood still, as if it did not want to follow the destiny of the others. I think I reached out my hand and spoke to it, although I didn't hear what I said. Maybe something like, Be good, brother animal.

2

The next day I returned to keep my father company. He was alone in a corner of the kitchen, beside the window. Actually, he wasn't alone, the room was full of children, five or six of them; but he was pensive, did not hear the voices around him, was crying perhaps: you couldn't tell from looking at his mouth. I asked him if he would like me to stay with him. He was already talking to himself, he raised his voice a little and I caught some words: ". . . but so beautiful . . ." then nothing more. I stayed around for a moment while he continued to talk quietly; I thought it might be better if I went out and looked for my brother.

I walked without thinking where I was heading, but now I know that an instinct was guiding me: my brother couldn't be far from the house. In fact he was very near, by himself, spading some ground, his head lowered and looking very weary. I stopped a little way from him and didn't speak. I felt he had been waiting for me and had sensed my presence. He left off working and remained that way for a moment, head bent down, without a word, as if lost in thought. Then he said to himself but in a voice loud enough for me to hear also: "Got to find a photo." He took out a wallet he had in the pocket of his corduroy pants—he never carried his wallet but he had it on him that day—and withdrew a packet of small photographs. He squatted on the ground. I sat down beside him.

"That one—she's in shadow," he said, handing me the first one. It was a family group, we were all there, my mother was the last on the left; you could see her mouth was smiling but her eyes were hidden by a shadow. It was a picture taken in the courtyard which is surrounded by elms. But who knows, it could also have been a suddenly cast shadow, a bird, a cloud, whatever. The fact remained that of my mother you saw nothing except the smile, like a pure spirit. The eyes had to be guessed; the hair, grey, evaporated into the background.

"This one here with the kerchief," my brother said, handing me the second photo. I looked at the photo, holding it by the edge with two of my fingers. This time the eyes were there. It was a very clear photo; yet even in this one something essential had been lost, because my mother's face was nothing more than the eyes and the smile. There was nothing else, even though it was all there. You couldn't see her hair because it was covered by a kerchief knotted tightly under her chin and also hiding part of her forehead and her cheeks. I tried momentarily to imagine her face in that photo without the kerchief; I saw only a mask.

"These ones are very little," my brother said, handing me three or four of them in reduced format. Indeed, you couldn't see much, not only because the photos were small but because the people—here was my mother, there was the whole family—were very far away, barely recognizable. My mother was always the last one over, to the right or to the left, as if she had joined the group timidly and, in a sense, still remained outside of it, apart. Being there, but not getting in the way. You couldn't make out her face very well, all the while you imagined her smile, that smile. It was impossible to get an enlargement of a photo that small and that out of focus: you had to first make a negative from the original and something was bound to be lost in the process—a little of the contrast between light and dark—; then you had to enlarge the photo from the new negative, and still more was going to be lost in this process—the last vestige of contrast between light and shade—, so that ultimately nothing would remain of the shade in the picture; you would find yourself before a face of pure light, an insubstantial nothingness, like air.

"This one's torn," said my brother, handing me the last. One corner happened to be bent and just in that corner, naturally, there was my mother. The fold had cracked the film of plastic that covered the front of the photo. My mother's face had so to speak disappeared, and you had to reconstruct it from memory by turning back the little crack inside the bend.

I returned the photos to my brother.

He shook his head as though in answer to an inward question, and resumed working again, in silence. I remained seated where I was, and without meaning to, I set to thinking.

So strange. We didn't have even one photo of my mother. That face I remembered in its least details, each wrinkle, each hair, nothing testified to its existence. It was no more. Of it everything was gone but the smile about the mouth and, in some pictures, the smile of the eyes. We had no way to reconstruct it, no point from which to start. The face that was the most known, the most present in our life, was, how should I put it? the least certain. We ourselves, her own children, we wouldn't have been able to say more than what those photos said: she was . . . she had a smile . . . and eyes . . . Nothing else. That is to say, nothing. We needed her in order to describe her. We were convinced that she would exist forever, like the world. The identical thought I had had the day before returned to me now: when we were born, she was there: she was part of the world, the whole world ought to have disappeared in order to take her away with it. It was unthinkable that you could save a single bit of the world—a fish, a leaf, a mouse—and not her. Our helplessness derived from an absurdity: that everything still existed except her. Had we been able to do something, we would have saved her at the expense of the world. We would have difficulty explaining to our children what she was like. Because now she was solely within us. We weren't in a position to point to a picture and to say, "Here, now you are going to see." We had nothing left but a memory, but a memory is personal, when you communicate it to someone else it stops being a memory—a face—: it becomes a word, almost nothing.

I thought, We are our mother. This thought contained neither pain nor joy.

I looked at my brother, now far off at the other end of the field, still spading, bent over, and that bent back hit me like a revelation: it was my mother's back.

I thought, He is my mother. That thought did contain pain.

I remained mutely in that pain for I'm not sure how long, but enough for my brother to finish the furrow and start back in my direction on the next. For some more time I looked at him, those bent shoulders, that tired and tireless way of moving arms and legs, like mountain people do. My mother didn't know how to make food tasty, she cooked the soup without salt like mountain people do, then each put in the amount of salt he wanted. To tease her my father sometimes told her, "You're from the hills," but it wasn't true and she would laugh. When she laughed, she put a hand over her heart. I never understood why. It seemed that she wanted to hold it still, as if laughing made it shake. Once instead of answering "Yes" to a question my father asked, she said "Why, of course" in perfect Italian and in a refined tone. My father looked at her dumbfounded. She burst out laughing and put her hand over her heart.

I set off before my brother got to where I'd been sitting. I would not have known what to say to him. I thought he would keep on working; instead he stopped and came with me, walking next to me. We got home together and went into the kitchen. My father was still there, in the corner. "Pa," my brother called. My father raised his voice a little and we could hear that he was saying ". . . but so beautiful." And that was all. While they were playing the children now and then bumped into him, but he took no notice. He was like a statue.

3

As I was about to leave, my brother put the little packet of photographs in my hand. I gathered he wanted copies of them. I felt uncomfortable, for a poor result was inevitable.

"They're not clear enough," I said. "Try to have them enlarged," he answered.

In the city I went into two of the fanciest camera stores, with the conviction that if they charged more, they were better. In the first, which was in the center of town, there were too many people, particularly old ladies who were still alive, with dogs on leashes. The light inside was subdued, bluish, so that looking in through the glass door you got the impression the shop was closed and the staff about to leave. Those few minutes, working hours just over, when the salesgirls stand about adjusting their stockings and making plans for the evening, and if you enter, paying no attention to you. But work wasn't over, that bluish light was on as in certain village cafés. I felt hostility upon seeing those ladies, useless yet alive. Why them and not my mother? I thought. By walking with a dog you live longer, they must have maids at home who die a little each day for them; someone must always die. I went out with the photos still in my pocket. I veered to the right, taking the street toward the railroad station. I don't know why, but after a few steps it occurred to me that on this street, opposite a big bookstore, there was another camera store, a very expensive one, I seemed to remember, and therefore surely a very good one. And indeed, there it is, brightly lit. There is a young woman sitting on a stool behind the counter. She has a saucer in front of her and an apple in her hand. She picks at the apple with little nibbling bites, like a rabbit. On the saucer is a chunk of mozzarella and a fork. The girl smiles at me, that smile looks to me like a request, I don't understand why but I am pleased that someone should ask me for something. She continues eating with her little bites, barely opening her mouth, biting at the peel and sucking upon it. Now I understand the smile: she is asking me to be kind enough to let her finish her snack. She could have asked me a lot more, today everyone can ask me a lot more for I too have something to ask in return, and I ask it: My mother is dead. Then I notice that what I have asked is not a request, it isn't anything. The girl eating the apple hasn't even heard; therefore I obviously haven't even spoken.

When she has finished eating she smiles at me, and I feel pleased that she has smiled. She slips down from her stool, she is standing. As best I can tell, she hardly has the strength to do what she does: remain seated, stand up, smile, walk to the trolley stop, get on and remain standing for ten minutes, get off the trolley and climb the steps to where she lives, eat some skimpy food and a fruit, comb her hair and come back again. That must be what her life is. I put the photos on the glass counter and ask if an enlargement can be made. She takes them one after another and passes them for a moment under a lamp; then she places them to one side, retaining only the last one.

She says, "My congratulations on the lady, she is very beautiful." She slips the photo into a white envelope and asks me my name. Believing it is my name I am saying, I give instead the name of my mother: "Elena." "Ready on Saturday, come before twelve." The other photos are in a pile, I put them in my pocket, but I sense there has been a mistake and the mistake is in some way bound up with that name,

Elena. I echo her "Saturday," and at the same time take the white envelope and open it. Inside is a photograph, the one the girl chose. I look and do not recognize her. My mother is very young, it is a photo taken at the time of her marriage. I slowly turn it over and on the back there is a stamp: "Headquarters . . . Regiment . . . Infantry . . ." The number of the regiment is illegible, it was poorly stamped on. It was the photo that my father, before he was my father, took with him into the army. Perhaps he looked at it every night. It's a very beautiful photograph, I mean the woman in it is very beautiful, "Congratulations." She has a round white face, a luminous gaze, two eyes that catch the light from everywhere around and the light makes them stand out as if they were the eyes of a statue, but painted. I happen to know that my mother's eyes were blue green, but I have the feeling that anyone could tell that just from this photograph.

I had never seen this photo: my mother before she was my mother. I shall never succeed in saying what I experienced. It was as if someone not yet born were walking down the street and someone else said to him, See her? You will be born from this woman. Congratulations, then left him there to look at his future mother, but who for the moment is a woman like any other—if he loses sight of her he'll never find her again. So it is the girl who will be my mother. There is a detail: she is wearing a hat, dark, with a broad curved brim and a light-colored ribbon running around it joins the brim to the high crown, following the shape of her head. The brim ought to create a shadow but instead her face is in full light. I mean to say that it was lit from below. She is not smiling, her mouth is serious, as if attentive. It's natural that one say, pretty much aloud, It's my mother, and I do say it, too, but the girl is now eating the mozzarella with the fork, taking tiny mouthfuls; she hasn't heard my words, therefore I haven't spoken, that's normal: the future child who walks through the streets and calls to his future mother isn't heard either. I recall having spoken the name Elena, but this is her real name, the one we never used because we all called her Neni. Why had I said Elena? In a way, I had indicated her maiden name as if I knew that her photo—the one photo that had been accepted for enlargement in a city shop—could not be a photo of Neni. It seems to me that everything is all right, that there is nothing else to add. I hand back the photo and say, "Three copies, please." I notice that the voice is not mine, that I haven't said the first words, but only the last, "please"; it does not matter, it's all right that way.

4

Saturday I return to the shop and wait my turn. It's crowded although there are no more than three or four people ahead of me, but that's too many in a shop that small. I look for the saucer on the glass counter, but it isn't there. The salesgirl is standing up, slender and fragile, moving her eyes slowly as if to conserve her strength. I sense that she recognizes me, I nod to her, but I wait my turn. The girl bends, opens a drawer, runs her fingers along the tops of a row of envelopes containing photos, she pulls one of them out and places it on the counter. I look at the

26

name written on it in ink, "Elena"—whoever that may be. Now it's the turn of a rather elderly lady who is going through a batch of color photographs, telling the story behind each one, where it was taken, who the children are, the tallest one isn't anything, he just happened to be walking by. I try unsuccessfully to listen to her. When she speaks she turns to this side and to that, wanting everyone to listen. Once she turns toward me also, but it's as if my presence were disturbing her, when she sees me she stops talking, then moves a little distance away and inspects her photos in silence. The salesgirl pushes the "Elena" envelope in front of me and smiles thinly. I'm not sure what to do. Then it occurs to me that it is I who said that name, I was unable to say "Neni" because it's not Neni, it's the young lady who will be my mother. I open the packet and look: it's not even that young lady, she doesn't even look like her: it's a girl wearing a hat with a wavy brim, a white face that you can't see because of the quality of the paper, opaque and absorbent. The eyes are two light-colored spots but without light. I turn the photograph over, the stamp from the infantry regiment isn't there. This woman seems a stranger, for an instant I have the sensation that I might have been born from another. On the envelope is scrawled 12,000. I leave the 12,000 lire on the counter and go out. It seems to me that the lady who was commenting on her photos was waiting for just that because she moves back to her place and starts talking again; but now I am in the street and no longer hear.

As I walk I look at the women going by. Not one resembles the one I have in my pocket, they are all equally alien to me, I have not yet been born from any of them.

In all this there is neither anguish nor pain, but something stronger. I stop behind a column and look at the photo; I don't know whether I'll show it to my father.

5

I meet my father on his way home. He went out to work but ended earlier than usual. He has a cat in his arms. This gives me an opening for conversation: I ask him where he found the cat, he shakes his head and continues walking without saying anything, the cat hugged against his chest as if he were warming it. We enter the house together, he goes straight into the kitchen; in a corner there are three or four cats lapping at a saucer of milk, he puts the new cat down and it immediately starts lapping away too, its fur ruffled from fear. It is a stray, skinny and soaking wet from having spent the night out in the damp. It takes two or three laps at the milk and begins to vomit, as it sneezes its sides draw in and its rib cage protrudes: were it not warm and indoors it would die this morning in some ditch, under some stump. Cats are ashamed of dying and hide themselves to do it. The littlest of the children running about in the house squats beside the new kitten and smooths its fur with a little spoon. Then he picks it up and brings it to my father who gets up from his big chair and with the dustpan digs around in the embers of the fireplace, puts the kitten in and covers it with some handfuls of ashes. The animal is uncertain, it doesn't know what to do, but in the meantime the warmth is reaching it and it feels better, it settles down comfortably and my father covers its flanks with warm ash. The animal stays there quietly and closes its eyes. A little later it is heard purring noisily, like someone with lung trouble.

I show my father the photographs. He looks at them, squinting his eyes and moving his head to and fro as if to say they won't do. He doesn't like them, or he doesn't recognize them. My brother comes in and washes his hands in a basin, he dries them with the old towel hung on a nail, he sees the photos and looks at them. He shakes his head.

Mealtime comes around, there is more food than usual on the table. My father complains about this, muttering his displeasure. He eats, as always, wearing his beret. No one speaks. The cat buried under the ashes in the fireplace smells the food, opens its eyes and moves under the table. My father puts it on his knee and feeds it from a spoon, then caresses it, stroking its back. The animal closes its eyes, ecstatic. "Found him in the ditch," answers my father, although no one has asked a question. "I don't want him dying. Watch out, whoever lays a hand on him." Saying that, he glances at the empty place where my mother used to sit. When my mother was alive he never looked there. Sometimes they argued, but usually they ignored each other, each one thinking his own thoughts. They used to sleep on opposite sides of the bed because my father was always cold and my mother was always warm. In the summer my mother used to bring an electric fan into the room, plug it in and set it upon a chair, aiming it toward her side of the bed; then she would stretch out, her shoulders bare, and fall asleep instantly. The doctor used to say that she could get sick that way, but she didn't worry about it. Once, no one knows upon what occasion, she had to have some chest X-rays. The radiologist turned on the machine and asked her, "When did you have pleurisy?" She shook her head indicating never. The doctor insisted, "How many years ago did you have this pleurisy?" She continued to shake her head, no. The doctor, who had come down from the platform and taken off his lead apron, got angry; he put the apron back on, put the lights out and remounted the platform. He relit the X-ray apparatus and looked. "You can still see the traces," he said, "it couldn't have been long ago. Where were you hospitalized?" My mother shook her head. The doctor wrote "Traces of pleurisy" on his card and dismissed her. None of us was aware that Mama had had pleurisy. Typhus, that we knew, just after she was married, she had had typhus; I was not born then but I heard it many times from my father. He used to say it was the improperly cooked food, my mother did not know how to cook, she preferred working in the fields, but after twenty years she was still defending herself against the accusation, saying that it was the fault of the new water, that in the new village she had moved to they had put in a pump at a depth of twenty feet and brought up tainted water, full of germs. To give added force to her words, my mother, raising her finger, cited a maxim in Italian, "Beware the changing of water." Regarding the early years in my parents' marriage I knew only three things: typhus, the wheel that doesn't turn, and the wet bag on the shoulders. The typhus belonged to my mother, the non-turning wheel and the bag were my father's. One day when the larder was empty, without even flour, my father went to the mill to have them grind a hundredweight of grain. The mill was about three miles away in another village. He loaded the sack of grain in the wheelbarrow and left. He returned at noon with a sack of flour. Throughout the whole journey, coming and going, the wheelbarrow's wheel hadn't turned, the rim of iron that encircled it was entirely worn away. This was my father's advice to anyone who thought he was engaged in a wearisome task: "Try going to the mill with a wheel that won't turn." The bag on the shoulders was the umbrella of the poor, protecting the lungs like the capes of the Great War. On a rainy day that God had ordained as one when my father had to work out in the open, he covered his shoulders with a bag; but after half an hour the bag was soaked with rain and instead of protecting him, it bathed him even after the rain had stopped—and that evening when he had finished working and had gone home, he sat himself down by the fire and ate three times more than usual. This was my father's advice to anyone who lacked an appetite or had a headache: "Spend a day in the rain with a wet sack on your shoulders, and you'll see how rapidly your appetite returns." Then my father went off to war and none of us at home had much appetite. From the store we bought only bags of broken rice. Once the storekeeper asked me, "Hey, don't you ever buy regular rice?" There was someone else in the store and he looked at me. From that time on, before going in to buy the broken rice, I waited at the door until the other customers had left and the shop was empty. My father was sent home when he got sick—although they would have had to send him home anyhow because his fourth child was born and Mussolini had a law that gave this bonus to heads of large families. The fourth child was a little girl. It was recommended that I look at her from a distance so I wouldn't transmit any germs by breathing on her. I had tiptoed up and breathed into her face. I wanted to see if she closed her eyes. Someone picked me up and carried me outside. My mother had turned white. My little sister had the little face of a cat, the nose of a cat, the mouth of a cat. Perhaps I could fit my hand right around her neck; with cats I was able to.

6

I spent a few days in the city, sleeping in my own house and looking out the window at people, searching for something but I was unsure what. What I saw was reflected in me as in a mirror, impersonally, indifferently. You meet hundreds of people and not one of them sticks with you. For whole days then I stayed in the house, looking at objects and trying to recognize them, as if their function had changed; I asked myself what the telephone is for, I will no longer hear her voice. But I never did hear her voice on the telephone; and yet something was going on which my mind could not grasp. Even now I am not sure, but it was as if I was hearing her voice in every voice I heard. I have a girlfriend here in the city and once when introducing her to German friends I said "Meine Mutter" instead of "Meine Frau" and she was very upset. The fact is that I lived knowing that she was there—]and now I must change my life. I have sometimes thought I was afraid of suddenly finding myself exposed, as if bereft of the presence of the preceding generation, the one that had begot me, vouched for me and for the whole of my generation: between us and death that older generation stands, screening us, so that death cannot see us and we cannot yet die. A strange thought, and yet it is very likely true—but I am unable to keep inward hold of it, as if its premises were false: I cannot die, I am firmly convinced that in the certainty of my death there must be some error, an error that I will take care not to commit. When I read of someone's death . . . I realize that I am starting to talk about the death of others, but at that point I needed to not think of my mother anymore. When I read of the death of someone I knew, I pause over it for a moment, look for the error, I find it, and I pass on—: that person made a mistake, it is proper that he die.

A manufacturer, fifty years of age, has died; his son was a pupil of mine, he used to come to school accompanied by a chauffeur and two bodyguards, former prize-fighters whose job was to prevent a kidnapping. But there was an error in his life, it was the enormous wealth that prevented him from living. One night every week he went to the race track, accompanied by two private guards, he bet the limit on the first three or four races, then hurried off, stopping at the window to collect his winnings. He used to wear nothing but white. He was a phantom. I always thought that he was bound to die, he had no other out, he was already dead. It was like that too with the university professor who had been my teacher, and who had refused an offer of promotion in another branch of work because it would have meant losing touch with the students. I've always suspected that he did so in order to retain the right to a triple raising of his coffin: the coffins of professors are raised three times in the courtyard of the University before being carried away on the pall-bearers' shoulders. Whenever I would meet him I seemed to see him already laid out horizontally, raised and lowered three times. He was already dead, there was that error in his life. But in mine there was no error. It wasn't lived with a view to death, and I couldn't understand how it could come about or why I would one day have to die. The image comes to my mind of that child I saw dragging his dead dog across the courtyard, crying because he wanted to play some more, he wasn't finished, and he begged it to stop dying. I would not have said "I am immortal," because this does not express what I think. I am a living person and I am unable to think that I shall ever not be one anymore. To this way of mine of being alive my mother also belonged, she was to belong to it forever, I would like to ask her to stop dying, but perhaps in her death there is an error on my part, on ours, on the part of all of us who love her; and it behooves us to remedy that error, to recall her to life, not to resign ourselves. They have told me that my father sleeps alone, otherwise she won't come back to rejoin him. But she has to be something more than just an illusion, she mustn't walk about only at night, she must be something we can see and touch, something real and, for those who love her, something . . . I do not know how to say it. I do not seem able, in this new world of mine of the city, to reconstruct and permanently maintain the image of her face, something to contemplate. In their old earthen world I think my father and brother are toiling to the same end. They can perhaps invent something. Their world has created everything, mine has no imagination, it is not able to transcend death because it is not made for the needs of humankind. Which are endless.

7

I went back to them but I found no one in the house, which was wide open and deserted. I went to look for them in the fields and sat down under an arbor. I saw them moving in a cluster, far off, upon the horizon, and I could not make out what kind of work they were doing. Certain tasks here are still done as they were in the old days, but the gestures and movements that once seemed so natural to me, I no longer understand them now, they seem no longer valid. There must be a visitor amongst them, a stranger, because I see a figure that remains upright, never stoops, is therefore not working. When noon sounds I see them straighten up, slowly because of the arthritis, then come toward me as they head home. My father is the last, checking the work just done every step of the way. The stranger moves right alongside him, as if he were going on telling him something of great importance. When they are near me one of them raises his hand a little and then lowers it. It is a greeting. I walk with them. On the way home we pass a small crossroads where a dirt road intersects one made of gravel, and in the middle there is a triangular patch of green with a tree in the center, an elm. The stranger goes over under the elm and spreads his arms; he doesn't say anything, he looks down at the ground. My father is beside him, he also looks at the ground. There isn't anything on the ground. The stranger turns this way and that, finds a stone and brings it to the middle of the green under the tree. My father sees another stone, lifts it with both hands and carries it to the same spot. "Here," says the stranger pointing with his hand. I recall that upon this spot there was once a low stone wall; the peasants, when in need of stones, had removed the wall piecemeal. "Where was it?" my father asks in Italian. "There," replies the stranger, lifting his arm. Every time he moves an arm or a leg, we hear a rustling, because he is wearing a corduroy suit and the wales of the fabric rub against each other. My father is looking for another stone, finds it farther off, in the grass, and places it exactly at the place indicated.

The stranger stands with his legs apart as if lost in thought, then takes four long steps the way peasants do when they want to measure off so many yards, two in one direction, the other two perpendicularly. His cap is pulled down low over his eyes, I cannot see his face. My father is attentive to the point of painfulness, something important must be going on but I don't yet know what. While the stranger has halted on the last point of his measurement, my father moves to occupy the starting point, and the two of them kick their heels into the ground and, twisting their feet, each makes a hole. My brother appears with a couple of stones in his arms, he found them in a ditch. He gives one to my father and one to the visitor, who place them at their feet. Finally a kind of square emerges, marked on the ground by the angle formed with the two stones that were deposited first right under the elm and by the sides, each two yards long, that end one with the stone by my father's feet, the other on the shoes of the stranger.

Everyone is silent for a while, standing with his head bowed. I see that someone is finally going to say something, I expect it will be the stranger. He raises his head and looks all around, then stares at the road and tells his tale. "I was running that way, they were shooting from a car, shooting out the windows and singing. She was sitting here in front of the wall.

When I turned the corner she saw me and jumped right up. She said to me, 'Back in here, in here, hurry,' fluttering her hands. I run over, I'm out of breath, I drop down behind the wall. The car arrives, comes round the curve and passes; they were singing and shooting into the air. After the curve, since they don't see anyone, they screech to a halt and back up. 'Where did he run to?' one of them wants to know from the lady. I do not hear her answer, I figure she has pointed in some direction with her hand. They tear off, the tires screeching. I wait a while, to make sure, then I come out. The lady isn't there anymore, a peasant rides by on a bicycle and tells me, 'They took Neni away.' "

This incident was new to me, it must have occurred at a time when I was little and my father was away in the army. From those days I remember only one morning when I wake up and there are two Germans in my room, helmets on their heads. One is holding a machine pistol and the other a bayonet which he jabs into each piece of clothing hanging in the clothes cupboard. My mother had a new dress bought two or three years before, and the German spoils it by poking it full of holes. I always assumed he had done it out of spite, and that was why the other kept her from moving, and she was clasping her hands—I didn't know then that my mother was helping some-one against the Germans. Then my father was sent to the front and he saw a Slav die. He cried all night, then, when no one was looking, all by himself he gave himself an injection of dirty water in his right knee, got on the sick list, and was sent home.

When she clasped her hands, she did it in a clumsy way, holding her palms apart, but instead touching the tips of her fingers together. She had square hands, large ones, with the skin red and chapped along the back, the palm hard and with deep furrows. She walked a little crooked, always hurting in one leg or the other. When she stood up she would make an effort and say "Oïe—oïe—oïe," three times, all in one breath. Her pension began after a three years' delay, she was able to collect it at the post office not every month, but only once every two months, and the amount equalled two days' pay for a worker, but she was happy as could be and once she had the money, she went to one daughter and gave her part of it and then to the other and gave her part of it, and with whatever was left she would buy herself a handkerchief or the yarn to knit herself mittens or a pair of stockings. So retirement pay for her actually meant a handkerchief every two months. She went to Mass on all the holy days and took communion. Going and coming from the rail she held her hands together, but at the moment of receiving the Host, she placed her arms in the form of a cross, touching her left shoulder with her right hand and her right shoulder with her left.

She walked with her head bowed. She always wore

a dark kerchief on her head, tied under her chin. On Saturday she would eat early in anticipation of the prescribed fast. Since the Church allowed you to drink, on Sunday mornings she drank a little water from a tin can kept tucked in among the ashes of the fireplace. The water was always warm and drinking it she tested it carefully with her tongue; if she detected the tiniest bit of ash, she spit out the whole mouthful, for there was the danger that the ash might break her fast.

8

Some days she came home so late and so tired that she had neither the time nor the strength to prepare supper. On those days she would cook only polenta, and would eat polenta and sugar. But she would take just the crust, the skin that forms on top of polenta when it cools; she would divide it into rectangular pieces, put a pinch of sugar inside each, then fold the corners up to form a cone. She would eat five or six of these cones with great appetite, then she would rest in the shade. Once she was in the midst of eating when a beggar came by. In her left hand she was holding the little cones of polenta skin with the dash of sugar, taking them one at a time with her right hand and putting them into her mouth. She was sitting in the courtyard, on the ground, her back against the wall of the house. Seeing the beggar standing in front of her, she smiled at him and stretched out her left hand, open, as if to offer him all it contained. He bent over the hand with an air of suspicion, peered uncertainly for a long moment, then took two cones and swallowed one. In his mouth the sugar dissolved, turning to liquid and running over his tongue. Some like that, some don't. He didn't. He dropped the other cone and, mumbling something, went away. As he walked under an arbor, he pulled off a bunch of grapes, and chewed some to get a better taste in his mouth. My mother watched with sorrow as he left, then, after some effort, retrieved the polenta from where it had fallen and ate it before it could get dirty. These movements wearied her, for she had pains in her spine. And this time too, with each effort she repeated an "Oïe," with each puff of breath.

My brother at that time was in the fifth grade and learning poetry by heart. One evening he recited the ballad of Albion and Rosamond, and ended it with a loud
    "Bevi, Rosmunda. Non piu parole.
                        Cosi si vuole."
    Bevea Rosmunda, ma con lo sguardo

> parea dicesse: Re longobardo,
> se la vendetta qui non mi langue,
>> berro il tuo sangue.*

My mother was there, heard it all, and left the house horrified. My brother was very proud of himself: he felt that he was finally learning grown-up things. Seeing our mother leave, or rather run away, it seemed to him that he was learning things beyond our mother's understanding. He looked about him victoriously, and his gaze halted upon me. I looked in the direction of the door.

In autumn, when the days shorten suddenly, so as not to lose time, she didn't bother coming home to eat at noon. She ate what there was in the fields, mainly fruit.

She would walk along the hedge bordering the fields looking for food, and what she found she would put in the kerchief she had taken off her head. She would fold the kerchief so it formed a little pouch, then with that little pouch she would go off to where the grass was tallest, there she would squat down and chew slowly, in silence. Her meal over, she would smooth out the kerchief with her palm,

---

* From a poem by Giovanni Prati (1815–1884). "Drink, Rosamond. Speak no more. / I would have it so." / Rosamond drank, but with her eyes / she seemed to say: Lombard King, / if vengeance is not denied me / 'tis your blood I'll drink.

put it back on her head and knot it under her chin, lifting her face to do so.

She had an impressionable spirit—she liked unusual things, discoveries, Italian words she succeeded in understanding, surprises. She never wanted presents. If she received a parcel with a gift, she didn't even want to open it; someone else had to do it, as a kindness. She would watch, sulking a little, her lips compressed and shaking her head. The more expensive the present was, the more upset by it she would be. She did nothing to keep her disapproval from being noticed. She immediately wanted to know how much it had cost, and she would inquire to find out whether the family of the person who bought it was all in good health. It always seemed to her that you couldn't buy presents without neglecting food, clothing, health. If someone in the world is getting presents, there must be someone else going hungry.

From March to September she went barefoot. The soles of her feet were thick and hard as leather and deeply creased. In the creases pebbles, little bits of grass and splinters would lodge. She extracted them with a needle, one by one, in the evening before going to bed, standing a candle on the floor and sitting down next to it.

9

While our father was a soldier we used to feel lonely in the evenings. After dinner she would have us gather around the hearth and she would tell us what she knew. In my opinion she also made things up. Usually they were stories about the saints. Her olden times way of inventing and telling was the people's way, but it was powerful. She aided herself with her right hand, using solemn gestures like those the priest uses when he explains the Gospel. That probably was the model she copied. She would start out by looking around for a subject and you understood that not even she knew what she was going to be talking about. She would say, for example, "Tonight," and raise her right hand, with the index finger up. She would then lower her hand.

"I am going to tell you"—she would raise and then lower the hand again—"about St. Teresa"—the hand remaining up and the finger extended. There was a great silence. Anyone who hadn't yet pulled his chair up did so quietly, sat down, drew up his legs and placed his feet on the seat so as to have his knees at the same height as his face; leaned his head against his knees, and wrapped his arms around them. We watched from beneath our brows. My brother was always caught with a mouthful in his mouth, but this was probably because he was continually eating even though there was never anything to eat. Ecstatic, he would gaze at her with his big eyes, blue like hers. He would stop chewing and the motionless mouthful would swell his cheek out for half an hour.

10

During the war she used to bake little unleavened flatbreads and the more they baked, the harder they became: it was like swallowing pebbles. Then we discovered the advantages of eating them raw, when the dough was soft and moist. Little bits of dough would remain stuck to her hands, and when she passed near us she smelled of flatbread. *Fugazza* is what we call it in our dialect. I had once seen a postcard which, so it seemed to me, pictured a mountain called Pian delle Fugazze. I had just learned how to read, and I imagined that in the country shown on the postcard the people had *fugazze* that were baked, sweet, fluffy, big as mountains. It had to be a foreign country that wasn't fighting a war. We

Italians were fighting a war against the world, that was why we had nothing to eat. You had to stay out of this war, no matter what.

Some peasants had refused to go and they were in hiding. They were never caught. From that time on the draft notices were delivered by the police, in pairs and armed, riding motorcycles and with lots of extra ammunition, and they insisted the draftees leave there and then. They came into our courtyard and asked in Italian where Mr. So-and-so happened to be. We children had never heard of anyone by that name. It was our father. He arrived, pale. He got into his other clothes. My mother was thunderstruck at his getting into those other clothes and at his compliance. Dishevelled, her lips bloodless, she kept asking, "You're going? You're going?"

She could not believe that a man would go off to war simply because they forced him to. That scene struck me like a revelation: my father was not the strongest one in the family, my mother was. I had seen my father, like Ursus, immobilize a heifer by the horns. What would our mother have done?

Then I remember that my mother and father hugged each other in the middle of the road and there was no policeman in sight. Probably they had orders to step off a ways and give kinfolk a chance to talk, the way it's also done in prison when the prisoners have visitors. I remember that my father set out on foot, and the motorcycle followed him step by step, the motor idling, just as they do with a prisoner.

11

There was little to eat or drink. The grown men were in Greece, Albania, Yogoslavia, in Africa and in Russia; only children, women, and the aged remained in the villages. The fields filled up with red and green, witch grass and poppies. Hares came right into the house, pheasants visited the chicken coops. Wine was made from wild grapes, bitter as vinegar. We filled some demijohns and saw to it they lasted a long time. My mother did it this way: she took a bottle of wine and drank just a little bit of it, then she added water until it was full again. At every meal—one or two meals a day—she drank a glass of that watered wine and replaced it with a glass of plain water. It was perhaps a miracle but after a month tinted water was still coming out, a sign that the wine wasn't all gone. My mother would hold the glass up to the light, see that the liquid was pink, would drink it with relish, then sit down and bow her head. She was pensive, always thinking.

Sparrows used to sleep in the haystacks, so it was possible to capture them with nets. A large net (one of those used for fishing) was set up about three feet above the hay; then the hay was flailed with a pole. The frightened sparrows would come rushing out, fly about in the dim light and become caught in the snare without a sound. Fifteen, twenty at a time. You killed them with a quick bite on the head. But you didn't suck, their blood is bitter, with a gamey smell. And they always have lice between their feathers. You had only to pluck them and they were ready for roasting. We had to do this on the sly, for our mother would have none of it.

She shopped once a week, when a grocer came by with a cart drawn by a horse. It moved through the villages at a trot, stopping at the farms. The grocer carried the essentials: peanut oil, vinegar, pepper, rock salt, grating cheese, mustard, whole cloves, cinnamon, stick or ground, sugar, imitation coffee, the bags of rice bits, some canned goods, oranges, lemons.

No one bought pasta, every family had a *tórcolo* to make its own *bigoli* or lasagna. The *tórcolo* was a kind of press, attached to the end of a sawhorse; you put the dough into the cylinder, a plunger forced it out underneath in *bigoli* or lasagna form according to which discs you chose to press it through. While my mother was pressing, one of the children had to be sitting astride the sawhorse, otherwise the *tórcolo* wobbled. None of us ever wanted to do it because it meant sitting there for half an hour. For the sake of fairness, my mother had us take turns, one of us today, another tomorrow. That way nobody complained.

She would spread the rock salt upon the table and grind it by rolling a bottle over it. After rolling it this way and that the salt would be crushed fine, she would collect it in the palm of her hand and store it in a little bag.

We did not even buy butter, we made it with milk. All you had to do was halfway fill a bottle and then shake it for half an hour: the milk had become butter, lumps of it would fall out if you turned the bottle upside down. The cloves and stick cinnamon were put in wine along with peels from the oranges to make mulled wine. She would heat the wine in a pot and carry it to my father, who had trouble with his lungs since returning from the front. My father would hold a burning straw just above it, the wine would catch fire with a big blue flame. Then he would drink it, as protection against bronchitis.

She never paid with money, there wasn't any. She paid with eggs. On the day the grocery man passed through, she had us gather eggs from all the nests, the ones we already knew of and the ones still to be found. Each child went around with a little bag or basket, looking for nests in the ditches, the storage spaces, the haystacks, the hedges. We put all the eggs into a large basket. Before selling them to the grocery man she would check them one by one to be sure none had gone bad: she held them up to her ear and gently shook them. If the yoke rattled inside, the egg was rotten. The rotten eggs she set aside and later buried. She did not wish to cheat. The grocery man would arrive and set the price: the price was different each time, it depended upon prices in town, whether they'd been coming to buy a lot of eggs from him or not, but it also depended upon the season: when the hens were laying a lot of eggs, they were worth little, when they were not laying, the eggs were worth a lot. One day there came a lady, like those in the movies, she wanted some eggs for her sick child. She came in a car, got out, and went into the house to talk with my mother. I looked at the car: it was brand new, shiny, and smelled slightly of gasoline. The engine had leaked two or three drops of oil, I touched them: the oil was warm, even the ground underneath the engine was warm. I walked all around the car and returning to the engine I saw written in raised letters the name of the owner: Fiat.

*   *   *

She washed the plates and the spoons with sand. She had a mountain of sand outside the front door and would come with her basket of dirty dishes and a gallon can of steaming water. She would wait a little until the water wasn't so hot, testing it every now and then by sticking her finger in. She would withdraw the finger and hold it in the air a moment, focusing her attention on it to decide whether or not she had burned it. She had large, stubby hands, almost square. She would begin to wash, slowly, patiently, wetting the plates and spoons, then sprinkling them with sand and rubbing them with the palm of her hand and the tips of her fingers. Then she would rinse them.

She never burned herself. She warmed the beds with coals she drew out of the fire with her fingers and put in the warmer. Sometimes the coals seemed out, covered with a black film. But she tested the ashes nearby to feel if they were warm; they were warm, so she took the coal in her hand, held it in her palm and before putting it in the warmer, blew upon it. She revived it in this way, and with the air she blew, avoided burning herself.

We went to bed sliding our bodies between two layers of warmth, sheets heated above and below. We turned red, we sweated. During the night, the heat evaporated, we stayed cold. In the morning we woke up slowly, our blood sluggish from having gone from burning to frozen. We would look at the beams overhead where glistening little white icicles were hanging: they hadn't been there the evening before, it was the humidity that had frozen during the night. The first one of us to speak sounded funny to the others: your morning voice was always different from your evening one.

When it snowed we would be isolated: the snow would drift against the door, we'd be unable to open it, we couldn't even see the path leading out to the road and could no longer see the line between the road and the ditch. We children would look at the world through the window panes. The birds seemed frightened; the sparrows would walk upon the snow, stopping to peck at everything that wasn't white, and the birds flew about in flocks over the plain, disappearing and reappearing as if guided by some obsession. My mother put on two pairs of long stockings, then rubber boots, then goatskin gloves. She opened a window and swept the panes clear of snow with the palm of her hand. She polished them bright, breathing on them with her warm breath. Then she placed a chair under the window, climbed up and hoisted herself over the sill, and dropped down on the other side. She would find a spade and clear the snow away until the door could be opened. Then with her feet she'd trample down the snow on the path right out to the road. After that we would wait for the snowplow which was sent by the township; we heard it coming from far off, pulled by a tractor and followed by a swarm of children on foot or on bikes, advancing like an army of partisans come to liberate the town.

12

When I was little, I heard a child say to its mother: "Wash me but don't get me wet."

A man was about to kill a dog and his son begged him: "Kill it but don't hurt it." There is something there that I have got to learn.

A child was playing hide and seek with some others. He closed his eyes and believed that, that way, he wasn't seen. There is something there that I have got to avoid.

13

Workers get up at seven, peasants at five. The workers pass by at daybreak, swaying from sleepiness, on their way to the factories in the nearby cities, and they see the peasants, already up and about for hours, in the midst of pitchforking hay into the mangers for the cattle. It's warm in the stables, it's a humid warmth, and the windows are already misted because of the animals' breath. The cattle yawn while they're eating and when they yawn, they stretch their hindquarters, their tail, swelling the veins beneath the skin of their dewlaps. Customarily, while he is performing this chore, the peasant will be speaking in a low voice, as if reasoning with the animals. The old folks save this job for themselves, and they are always the first ones up. On a farm where you hear a cow lowing because it's hungry, that's the farm where you'll find a drunkard who has no respect for the earth, for bread, or for blood. Jesus Christ got down off the rump of a she-ass because he had spied a crumb of bread on the ground, and he picked it up so: he moistened the tip of his forefinger with saliva, touched the finger to the crumb which stuck there, and put his fingertip into his mouth. He did this to teach us that bread ought not to be left upon the ground, unless there be a line of ants there. Among us, the one who gets up first in the morning is always the father in the household, he is also the first to bend over to pick up bread that has fallen from the table.

The morning after the stranger came we hear the cattle lowing, so our father has not gone to the stable. We look for him in the fields all around—nowhere in sight. We finally find him at the crossroads where my mother had saved the stranger's life: he is standing there, erect, with his arms folded and gazing at the mark on the ground showing the position of the wall. We bring him back to the house and he is very pleased that no one has fed the animals yet. He takes the pitchfork and distributes hay in large amounts, upon it sprinkling handfuls of *ceroso,* a mash made mainly of ground corn, it would be like cake in a human being's meal.

It seems to me that he is singing under his breath, but I can't be sure. Maybe he is a little bit touched, or maybe he has accepted her death. And perhaps these two things are the same. It's not possible to think about death for very long without going a little crazy. So we are all a little crazy. This slight craziness is normal, and anyone who is not this way is not normal.

I don't know why, I have the feeling that my mother and the stranger were never able to talk to each other, because the stranger spoke Italian and my mother didn't know Italian. She was truly the least of all the things in creation, the poorest of all. I think that may be why I am writing about her, because if she is marked out by destiny for immortality (as my story shows) then anybody can be marked out for it, one only needs to be sufficiently humble. One evening my mother was combing her hair in the courtyard, she had very long hair, somewhat curly, and she used an iron comb because the ones made of bone cost more and break. She was combing it carefully because iron combs can hurt you; a woman who lived in the house across the way had given her scalp a scratch, she had said "Aïe!" and scratched the place with her fingernails—half an hour later she was unable to move her neck, and before night came she was dead of lockjaw.

When she finished combing her hair, my mother straightened up with a jerk so that her hair fell back over her shoulders, and it was the second and last time that she spoke Italian, exclaiming, "The stars are looking down on me!" My father gave her a worried and despairing look, but I was proud of her and wondered if she really knew how to speak Italian.

So she wasn't even able to speak with that man, it was as if she had saved the life of a black man, a Chinaman, a Tartar.

And yet it was an Italian, he lived in a nearby village and had heard that my mother had died and he had come to bear witness. That is the way it always is. For days, all anybody talks about is the person who has died, who has therefore never been more alive. Everyone has his own monument composed of spoken words and memories, but here no one knows how to write and the unwritten utterances are already effaced and the memories die with the death of those who remember: the death of a man in this part of the world where there is no written tradition is not only the death of that man, but the death also of all the dead kin that lived in his mind. In his turn, those who love him will remember him and will bear him in their memory. To go toward death is like walking hand in hand and forming a chain. Mankind will be just when that chain links all men together. Then history will be in a positive direction and have a positive meaning, that is, a collective one.

Before noon my father goes off to dig clear the foundations of that little wall, and almost at once he comes to them under the grass, and they turn out to be of stone, not of brick. He digs patiently, following the course of stones and ridding them of dirt and cleaning the grass roots even out of the cracks between them.

A square space emerges, smaller than the one the stranger indicated, and you realize that the stranger had felt this refuge to be much larger than it was in reality: the fugitive feels like an animal and seeks a small hole, his own size, too snug even for the hunter's eye to penetrate. The small square of white stones is incomplete, but at one place the stones are worn in a way that forms a smooth surface: the entrance was there. My father sits down at this entrance and looks out. Before him, two kilometers away, he has the campanile of the village; it is just visible above the expanse of fields, for it is not tall. It has two openings on each of its four sides. When the wind blows in its direction, the sound of the bells is carried away, you do not hear them; but if you look at the openings you see the bells swinging, mute. Lost in thought, my father looks and sees the openings close and re-open, close and re-open. He looks harder, because what he sees is not possible, and realizes that the largest bell is swinging from left to right, right to left, and there is an instant during which it covers the opening completely. The sun is straight over head. Therefore it must be mid-day striking. My father gets up and walks toward the house, his head down. After the meal, in order to move a full sack of grain that someone has left blocking the door, he is obliged to make a greater than ordinary effort. He has it in the air when he feels something give in his back. He lets go, the sack falls to the floor, the cloth splits and the grain flows everywhere, all around my father who is now on the floor too. We carry him to a couch that has been covered with burlap; it is set under the window, in the kitchen, near the hearth. He doesn't complain, he doesn't seem to be in pain. These things that go wrong with the back are common occurrences in the lives of peasants and workers who ask too much of their spinal column; while the opposite sort of thing happens to white collar workers, whose backs won't move at all. One by one my brother checks the rings along his spine, pressing each one lightly with his hand; each one seems to be in place. I lift my father's legs and stretch him out on the couch so that his entire body can be horizontal and rest. In doing this I grab his legs behind the knees, and it feels as if his right knee is wrapped inside a handkerchief. Those who in the course of their work kneel on hard surfaces wrap their knees. I uncover his right knee and look at it: there's no handkerchief, but around the kneecap is a cushion of blue flesh, soft and swollen: in short, his whole knee is inflamed, and we hadn't known anything about it. My father gestures irritably for us to cover his leg back up. Then the thought enters my head that I have seen that leg before, but I cannot remember when. My mother is dead, she is no longer there. Ah yes, when he came back from the army: he had been in the front lines and seen one of the enemy die, that enemy soldier who was dying and my father who had not fired cried together the whole night; then in the morning my father injected a syringe of water into his right knee, and with the knee swollen up that way he reported in sick. Had he been discovered, they would have killed him, my peasant father, and his country would have been ashamed of him; instead, he was judged unfit for service and sent home where his fourth child had just been born, and so he had a right to go back anyway. The syringe of water is a trick the soldiers were using a lot and the medical officers knew it, they would draw out the water and send the soldier into the front lines. But my father had already gone into the front line and when they drew the water out of him they found it was genuinely infected, he must have used contaminated water. At home he went around for a few days with his knee exposed, to dry up the swelling: his knee was big, round and blue-

green, like a watermelon, I hold it between my hands
with dismay, I think of my mother who had saved the
life of a stranger who did not speak her tongue and I
think of my father who not only had not fired at the
enemy, but to punish himself for a death which he
was responsible for—because he was a soldier—he
injected water into the knee that I was now holding
between my hands, round as a watermelon. I carefully cover it back up for him. My belief is that with a
little rest the swelling will go down. I think to myself
that none of the enemies from those days will ever
come to visit my father. The one who was dying that
night, died that night, and the others whom my
father never shot at won't ever know it. But they
stayed alive, and that's what counts. When others are
killing, you must save as many as possible. When the
others are dying, you must invent a form of immortality.

My father had that blue-green knee, my mother
had those big blue varicose veins standing out on her
legs, and chapped feet with deep cracks in them.
Rather than tasks that call for brief heavy efforts, she
preferred to do the lengthy tasks. She would never
abide by the time. In the morning she'd advance the
alarm clock so she could be out of the house before
anyone else, at noon and at the end of the afternoon
she pretended not to hear the bells in order to
continue working. Sometimes you had to force her to

quit. There was something mystical and tragic about her dedication to work, driving herself until her last ounce of strength was gone, up to the point of collapse. Then she would emerge from the field with slow, reeling steps, she would look for a little shade and sit down with an "Aïe," rather, she would not sit but sink to the ground, and would recuperate her strength, breathing rapidly and fanning herself with her straw hat. She would be smiling. Never again shall anyone smile like that.

I never heard her sing, or express a desire, or say "I want that piece of clothing." When the vendors came and unrolled their yardgoods, she would wipe her hands with her apron and feel the fabric, rubbing it between her thumb and forefinger; then scrunch up a corner of the piece in her closed fist, then open it and see whether the material went back to its original shape or remained wrinkled. If it smoothed back out, it was real wool; otherwise it was artificial. But she would apply this test just to find out, not with a view to buying, because at the end of her testing, when the merchant looked at her to see whether she was about to buy, she would shake her head in refusal and walk away. She didn't put on a sad look. She simply wasn't thinking about it anymore.

14

Once a foreign officer in uniform came with an automobile full of readymade clothes and an interpreter. He scattered the stuff all over the grass and ordered us to try it on, that is, he spoke angrily, first pointing to the heaps of clothing on the ground, then pointing at us children. He was much too excited for us not to obey. All of us undressed right there, I, my brother and my sisters, and we put on pieces of clothing, fishing them out of the pile. Since the officer was still acting nervously and walking up and down in the courtyard, even my mother, without undressing, tried on something, a kind of green-colored overcoat with a hood. She tried on that garment resignedly, like an innocent person who, free one minute, is put into jail the next. Her thick fingers struggled with the buttons. She had thick fingers, better suited for heavy work than for sewing. She was never able to thread a needle, she didn't see it well enough. She would hold the needle up high with her left hand and with her right the end of the thread, she would moisten it with her mouth, then try to insert it through the eye; she would miss by a quarter of an inch. Then I'd go up and thread it for her. She would take the needle, hugging it in the palm of her hand, then open her fingers and look for it; the needle's point was almost always stuck into her palm, but she had calloused skin, it didn't hurt her. The American officer wore eyeglasses and this made him appear even more awesome to us. Peasants cannot afford glasses, even when they can't see three feet ahead of them. There we were, dressed in foreign clothes and all in a line. My youngest sister got the wrong size, she was in an outfit that reached to the ground. The officer flew into a rage and with his stick—he had a stick like a cattle dealer's switch—he speared from the pile a little blue dress, for an infant, and held it out to her, letting it hang from the end of the stick like a fish. Although scared, my sister took it, removed what she had on and got into the new piece of clothing. I'm not sure what time of year it was but I remember that when she took off the dress, my sister was in just her panties for a moment and had goose bumps; so it must have been cold, but I'm not sure, since goose bumps also come from fear.

Now we were all in order, standing in a row, with clothes that fit and were new. The officer inspected us one at a time, satisfied. We couldn't make out what he wanted. Then the interpreter stepped forward. He spoke in Italian, he was not one of us. He said that we could buy all this for very little, we could also keep the clothes we were wearing now that we had put them on, all we had to do was pay first, and he named a price. I was very young, I didn't understand anything about prices; but in making the comparison, it seemed to me that all those clothes really cost very little, less than one article cost ordinarily.

My mother didn't know what to answer. She looked for any excuse, took a button on her coat and pulled it hard, trying to pull it off, doubtless so as to be able to claim that the buttons were poorly sewn on. The officer who was walking around slapping at his shoes with his stick, as do cattle dealers, saw the canny purchaser at work and came to a stop, becoming even more nervous. He was right in front of me. He was no longer slapping his shoes; he was holding the stick horizontally, across his chest, the handle squeezed in his right hand while with the palm of his left he caressed the stick's pointed end, polishing it, so to speak. He was raising and lowering the toe of his right shoe, and under the sole I saw—and can still see—a bit of straw that moved, as if alive. My mother gave a final tug, then let go of the button; it wouldn't come off. The officer's expression seemed to indicate relief, he fixed the pointed end of his stick in the ground, shifted his weight and began to rock his right knee backwards and forwards, all the while looking joyfully at the interpreter. He no longer looked as much like an enemy as before, we might even become friends, but I didn't dare leave my place in the line and I glanced at my mother with trepidation. I knew that she was unable to buy, we could never buy anything. The interpreter repeated the price. Now all of us children had our eyes on our mother. She lowered her head very slowly, remained still for an instant, then shook her head, without speaking. The officer's knee stopped rocking, I saw the end of his stick whip out of the ground and beat against his shoe. The interpreter moved languidly toward my mother, he seemed in no hurry and that made him belong to the master race; he halted in front of her and pronounced a figure, different from the first. I counted rapidly, it came to exactly half; I multiplied that number by two and got the number before. My mother still had her head down, without lifting it she indicated another no, slowly, and I thought I heard a sigh. With swift strides the officer returned to his car, got into the driver's seat; he slammed the door shut, thrust a cigarette in his mouth and lit it. Smoking, he looked at us through his glasses ironically or pityingly, which was the same thing. The interpreter appeared for a moment to be lost in thought, then barked out an order sharply and very loudly, which struck us as pointless amid all that silence: "Take 'em off." We began slowly to slip the buttons from their holes and to take off those foreign clothes, but without daring to put our own back on, for no one had given us permission to.

The interpreter gathered up all the new clothes in an armful, carried them to the car and got in beside the officer. The car drove off slowly and disappeared. My brothers began to get dressed right away, but I decided to look for that bit of straw that had been in contact with the officer's shoe. I picked it up and looked at it. It hadn't broken because, under the weight, it had sunk into the soft earth and in that way it had been preserved.

15

Some French missionary brothers call me and ask whether I would care to contribute toward the baptism of a child born on the same day my mother died, and to give it my mother's first name. They specify that this first name must be a nice one and be approved by the parents of the child. I gathered that all this was preparatory to asking me what my mother's name was. I provided it at once: "Elena." The brother who was talking to me seemed very pleased, his tone became one of joy: "Hélène, but of course! A lovely name. We will give it to a little African baby who was born that day. She is sure to

like it when she grows up." While I was listening to
these words I slowly took the receiver away from my
ear, as if unwilling to hear any more.

And in fact by the end I was no longer hearing.
Something like an error had caught my attention in
those words *Hélène, African*. My mother was not
Hélène, she was Elena; and she was not black, she
was always very pink. She didn't know the art of
using make-up, apart from a little brick-colored powder. She kept it in a small brass box on the mantel and
used it only on Sunday mornings when she got out
her holiday clothes to go to Mass. In the box there
was a wad of cotton with the powder underneath.
My mother would take off the lid, dip the cotton wad
and dab it against her cheeks, then she would shake
it clean of powder, and would smooth out the make-
up in such a way as to make it invisible. I believe I am
the only one in the world who knew of this sin of
vanity. Since the church was a half-hour's walk away
and since, no matter what the season, there was
always wind, not long after she left the house the
powder would be all gone and her natural color
would have been restored.

She aged very quickly. She became white. She
hadn't had even a day of real life, she didn't want to
resign herself to being old before being young. She
began by tinting her hair. Not being able to buy the
desired dye, she used some product she already had
in the house, dipping a little stick in it, then rolling

her white hairs around it or rubbing it upon them, those white hairs turning brown immediately. Probably she used tincture of iodine. So for a few months we had a mother with chestnut-colored hair, who didn't look like our mother. But she wasn't convinced by those results and shortly gave it up. Then she hit upon another idea: she ceased looking at her hair. She used a small rectangular mirror, the same one my father hung at the window by a string when he was shaving with his straight razor. In that mirror you could see only one part of your face at a time, one cheek or the other, this eye or that one, your forehead or your chin. When she was powdering herself she kept her cheeks in view, but before finishing with the mirror, she adjusted it higher in order to have a look at her hair; a glance was enough since she had already combed it from memory. The glance had become a habit. When she began to go white, she gave up even the glance and forever after ignored her hair, as if it were no longer a part of the human body. The veins in her legs swelled, they stood out like a network of roots. They seemed to come together into knots like the rivers on a map. So she got into the habit of wearing long woollen stockings that covered and hid everything. From then on she ignored that part of her body also.

She became stooped, and began to ignore her body altogether, as if it no longer existed.

*   *   *

Somewhere in the world there's been born a little woman Negro body that may be called Hélène and which may have some relation with the body of my mother. One day I may find out that Hélène has taken a trip, hurt herself, become married. But no, that would be worse, it would mean continual proof that it was not my mother, that no woman can ever be my mother. Because my mother never took a trip, was never hurt, never married. That last calls for an explanation, but I am not sure which one. She knew nothing outside her house and those places where she worked, but those places she knew by heart. A phrase comes to mind: what does a man do who spends his whole life shut up at the bottom of a pit? He places ants in a row and counts them. The pit hadn't always been the same one. In fact my mother changed houses around her twentieth year. Today, we called this move matrimony, and it's another thing entirely; above all, an expense. In those days you didn't spend anything, and it was also because there was nothing to buy. It's as if for many generations people, animals, and the earth lived together, without any things in the picture. Now it's the opposite: men and animals have become things, and the earth is entombed below. Today, to get hurt means to look after oneself. Then, it meant to wait until the hurt went away. In front of the house from time to time there would be someone who was doing nothing: he had hurt himself, or some hurt had come to him, now he was staying put, and waiting.

I write these things in Italian, that is, I translate them into another language. He who is denied the use of his own tongue cannot be happy and feel free. The more I write, the more I shackle myself. This book will be short because, at bottom, it is only an epigraph.

16

In the past, on the spot where my mother saved the life of the stranger, a public building must have stood, because that land where the two roads cross belongs to the township. Perhaps they had a dispensary there, one of those that open once a month: the doctor would come with a nurse and look at the seriously ill, brought in from the surrounding area by all sorts of means, hand-carts, gigs, carrioles. Or else he gave vaccinations. Or verified that the cured were completely cured. Something like this is still done in Yugoslavia except that the health service comes by once a week or even daily, and also brings medicine.

Now my father has uncovered the foundation of the little edifice and wants to rebuild it. He leaves early in the morning carrying bricks, stones, all the equipment he may need for mixing mortar and putting up a wall. He is doing it alone, he hasn't asked for help. He handles plumb line and level the way qualified masons do. He respects the ground plan of the former structure: he leaves a door where there was a door, opens a window in the wall facing south. From that window it will be possible to see the campanile.

He is happy, it is well just to let him go ahead. It seems that his knee has stopped hurting. One evening, the chores all finished, I have a look at it for him. It appears to be less swollen than usual, perhaps activating it has reduced the amount of fluid.

The construction is small, narrow, and low. If it was a clinic, there was room inside for only the doctor, the nurse, and the patient. The others waited outside, on the grass.

When you come to the roof, you have to have help. All of us in the family lend him a hand, the stranger shows up too, and there are also some volunteers from other households, people who knew her more closely. It is implicitly understood that this is a sort of monument to the dead woman, but not the usual monument they bring in and set up in every village square to commemorate the war dead: war, it's others

who wanted it, and they are the ones who provide
the monument, already built and inscribed, and they
plant it there as if in payment for the lives they took.
This one is a monument that we ourselves are making, for one of our own, because that person did
something we consider right. Each of us has in
addition personal reasons. My father is building it out
of love also, the love made up of innumerable mo-
ments that he will never be able to relate, and which
for that reason he is collecting together in these
stones, touching them one by one as if unburdening
himself. The stranger joins in in order to pay his debt,
but also in order to bear witness: each one of these
stones is restored to its precise place because he has a
precise knowledge of the place. We children work
because in this way we reconstruct our mother; and I
think continually—I mean there is not an instant
when I am not thinking about it—that in this way we
are finally making up for the lack of photographs of
our mother; instead of a snapshot of the moment
when she saved the stranger, we will have this
monument, which is something infinitely clearer,
and more ours. Suddenly I have another illumination:
it is right that this monument be built by a man who
wrecked his leg for the selfsame reasons the monument commemorates. I think with alarm that this leg
might get well before the construction is finished.
Then I am ashamed of my fear. I feel a pang in my
heart. But after a time I understand that one must be
worthy of approaching these stones and handling

them. In all of us there is something that resembles gladness.

We build the roof with beams, across the beams we nail boards and on the boards we align the tiles. Before too long the sparrows will be nesting under the tiles, and in that there is something right. Our mother will never be alone again.

After a few days the work is complete and we can look at it. We look at it from the front; my father is in front of everybody else, he being the one who can be nearest, and we're behind him. The stranger, without anyone asking him to, walks all around the edifice, then comes back to the place he started from, by my father's side, and nods approvingly, several times.

The edifice is in the center of a crossroads; every so often someone passes by, sees it, and pauses to look at it.

The old timers remember that this construction once existed in the past, compare it with their memory of it, find it identical, and go off nodding assent. Some words are needed above the entrance to recall the woman's name, her life. But my father is against it: no words. Because if words were written, they would have to be written in Italian, and this would be a betrayal. The best way is to explain everything to all those who inquire, speaking to them: spoken words are like the wind, which sullies not but sweeps all things away.

17

In two weeks' time the procession through the countryside will take place. It takes place once each season, in keeping with tradition. It is the occasion for blessing the crops in the fields and the sick in the houses; but it is awaited even by those who are not believers, for it serves to make known who is sick and in need, when these are things of which no one may yet be aware. The procession visits the entire village, all the sick are discovered and a rotation system is set up to care for them. It's odd how people here fall ill just on the eve of the procession. It's as if everyone were trying hard not to fall ill beforehand, because they know that no one would come to see them. On the eve, however, those with an incipient illness give way to it voluntarily, lose their strength, leave the door ajar, and take to their beds. The crowd will stop in front of the door and one or two people will go in to see what there is to be done.

The procession will last an entire day and will halt where possible near wayside altars. There the less seriously ill gather, those who are on their feet and able to go out of doors. And also the small children. When the harvest is blessed, they turn around to look at the fields, expecting the wheat to shoot up out of the ground all of a sudden.

Holy words and blasphemies give the impression of omnipotence.

Having an altar nearby is an advantage for those who are unwell. There isn't any altar near us and the people who need one have to go pretty far. My father says we could have put up an altar inside the monument, but we would have to have thought of that before, there's not enough time left now. This thought torments him, he feels he has done something wrong. He talks about it with everyone he meets, is even starting to go to their houses to sound them out. They all agree: between the different altars scattered here and there, this would be best of all; furthermore it would augur well: there where somebody was restored to life others might regain their health.

The priest consents, but first makes one thing clear: an altar cannot be raised in honor of, only in memory of. This is just what my father wanted: that the memorial belong to everyone, and that it serve some purpose, and that (here I will not be precise) it be holy. I wanted to put that in another way. He is filled with self-reproach for having let the time go by, he comes home with a lump in his throat and tears in his eyes. For a week he does not say another word about it, so that if before it was already too late, by now it's not humanly possible.

A week before the ceremony he has a dream: he sees the sick walking along the road in small groups, each group made up of persons with the same malady. The rear is brought up by the ones who have something wrong with their feet. Then these people disappear underground. They were seeking afar for an altar, in silence.

18

Early the next morning, at dawn, my father has a fever. It must be his leg, which is swelling up. He hasn't slept a wink all night. He doesn't eat, he goes down to the workshop, sits, and begins to look over his tools: hammers, pincers, tongs, tin-snips, cold chisels, saws, a mallet, the anvil, the hardwood hammering block. He eyes them the way an enemy eyes an enemy. He has the *ramina* brought to him, the large pot we use every night for cooking the polenta, it still has some crusts sticking around the rim. He rubs it gently with the palm of his hand, pensive. He inverts it over the hammering block; he reaches down a hatchet hanging on the wall. The pot is made out of thin sheet copper, but at the rim the metal has been bent back and turned under, and there it is thicker and tougher. He strikes a sharp blow with the hatchet and the roll of copper cuts like pulp. He strikes another blow, exactly opposite the first. He lifts the pot and with the tin-snips cuts it all the way through, squeezing the two halves together at the rim. The pot opens wide, like the skin of an orange. Outside the door he lights a fire with twigs and branches. With an iron stake he pushes the halves of the pot into the fire and leaves them until they are white hot. He puts on a work apron, takes off his beret as though he were in church, and feels his knee. It is swollen, it hurts, everything's all right. In the stable he collects a pan of urine, brings it back and places it in the middle of the workshop. From the fire he takes the two copper plates, oxidized by the heat; he watches them steam in the damp morning air, then thrusts them into the basin where they sputter like frying fish and shed their skin of oxidation. Now it is pure, soft copper, you can do what you want with it, it bends under the pressure of the fingers like willow bark. One can score it with a fingernail, for the fire has expanded it and rendered it supple. He cuts it into strips as a tailor cuts cloth. He takes the largest strip and tries it with his teeth—a little nip, like a cat's on the neck of a mouse, to be sure it is still alive. He puts the plate on the block and smooths it with his palm, then with the back of his hand. He stares at it and wonders what can fit upon it.

A little tree, or a spike of wheat, the Mentana variety, each grain with its little hair. Trees, everybody has trees; bearded wheat grows better around where we are because it has a short, tough stalk, it takes a storm to break it, wind and rain alone aren't enough. In other places they plant the Imperatore variety because it yields more grain and the spikes are bigger, but they haven't realized it's got a heavy spike on a slender stalk, and when the wind comes down onto the plain it flattens entire fields of it. The stalk snapped, the flattened wheat rots. If it manages to straighten up, it produces little—like a cripple, it can't get far. So he decided to put a Mentana spike on the copper and tried to visualize it. He picked up the piece of copper and, squinting, imagined, right in the middle of it, a spike of wheat with its beard. Something wasn't right, there was an error, but he couldn't tell where, he tried to get rid of it by shaking his head. Again he shut his eyes to visualize the spike standing up in the middle of the copper strip. The error was still there, you couldn't see just where. One by one he looked at the elements composing the stalk: the stem, a leaf—a single leaf was enough, might even be too much—, the two rows of grains, each grain in the husk, each grain tipped by its hair, two rows of hair. And still something was wrong. He sent a child to pick a stalk of wheat, Mentana, not

Imperatore, Mentana, and he sent another to fetch a pencil. With the pencil he drew a spike on the copper, the spike he had in his head. The pencil, much too small, rolled around in his hand, which was much too big; he kept trying to get the right grip on it. He made mistakes in the lines, would erase them with the tips of his fingers; would rub his rough skin over the smooth copper and there would be no more line, gone like a clod of earth disintegrated by the harrow. At last the drawing could be said to be perfect; but there was still that error which he couldn't identify. The stalk of wheat arrived, he placed it on the piece of copper over the drawing in order to compare hair against hair, husk against husk, grain against grain, stem against stem. But by chance that particular stalk of wheat had no leaves. Strange. The leaf must have fallen off, been torn off by the wind, by looking one could perhaps find some trace of it, or the still attached sheath. There was no sheath. The stem did have two or three leaves, but in tufts near the roots. Then there was half of a leaf, dangling. Above that the stem was smooth. Yes, that's the way it was. Mentana had no leaves under the spike, it was truly a plant designed to resist the wind.

He had grasped an important thing and, struck by that discovery, he dwelled upon it for a moment and immediately after he felt content, so content that he murmured, I thank thee. He asked himself who it was he had said thanks to. To thee, that was the answer while, almost smiling, he put his thumb upon the leaf he had drawn with his pencil and rubbed it away. What remained now was the true stalk, real, existing, artistic; he had only to engrave it. That called for a burin, even a chasing-tool, smaller and finer than a burin, in order to get precise lines. He looked for nails of various thicknesses, cut them with a pincers and filed their points so that they ended in a bevel. The ends of some he flattened with his hammer, tapping hard or lightly to thin them more or less, and thus got himself a set of engraving tools, fine, medium, and wide. He took one of the fine ones, set the cutting point on the pencil-line and lightly tapped the nail-head. He lifted his chisel and inspected the groove cut in the copper. It was a fine but deep groove that ran exactly through the pencil-mark into the metal. He tilted the chisel back a little and continued to tap it lightly with the hammer so that it just cut into the copper and moved along, following the pencil-mark. He did the entire stem in this way, then he changed chisels, taking an even finer one, and with that, tapping ever so lightly with the hammer, incised the outlines of the grains of wheat and bits of beard. At first he had the feeling he was bringing his effort to bear not upon the metal, but upon himself; he groaned, the fingers of his left hand were trembling so that before giving the taps with the hammer, he several times had to steady the point of his hand, that is, the point of his chisel. So as to make no mistakes on the metal, he decided to give himself a little rest, sat on the anvil and began to examine his hands. The shaking in his left hand was at the fingertips. He watched with a feeling of helplessness while they trembled: Don't shake, he prayed. To relieve the tension he looked one after another at the ring of children staring at him, their hands behind their backs as if awaiting orders. He couldn't tell who was who because with the mist over his eyes he couldn't see them distinctly. He rubbed his eyes with the back of his hand. His eyelids felt swollen with liquid. He lowered his fingers to the metal, pointed the chisel at the line; its point held still. He started in tapping again with very light blows, following the entire contour of the drawing, grain by grain, hair by hair. He felt as though he were working in the open fields, with the same inner joy. At length he took the sheet, went out into the sun, and looked at it: there wasn't much to be seen, and then this spike of wheat indented that way made no sense: exploring with his fingertips, all he felt was emptiness, not the round fullness of the grains. He had to think, and he sat down. The children didn't understand what was going through his mind, but they kept quiet because they knew something was amiss. Considering it from different angles, he kept turning the sheet with the engraved drawing, and finally dropped it altogether, like a reject: there was little time now, the procession was only a few days away, it would all take place as it had every other year except for the one most important thing: she wasn't there, instead of her there was nothing, she was truly dead. He pulled his knees up against his chest, lay his head upon them and stayed like that a long while until he found a consolation: he wasn't himself worthy of building this altar, that was why the copper wouldn't let itself be sculptured, and there was nothing further to be done about it. He actually heard these words, so he actually uttered them; and indeed he found himself upon his knees, his arms spread, and he was weeping as he spoke, as if he were already at the Last Judgment.

Lowering his arms, he touched the ground and felt the sheet of copper. Lifting it again, he passed his fingertips over it and, without realizing it, felt the raised surface of the image he had engraved there. Finally, the veil fell from before his eyes, and he saw those details in relief: the stem, the grains, the beads, all the lines stood out in sharp, clean, continuous relief, the light, encountering this relief, cast a faint shadow which rendered the stalk of wheat more real, more true, more present, more artistic: from it flour could be got, and dough kneaded for the Host.

It was a miracle, how it had come about there was no knowing. He turned the sheet over, then over again, his eyes ever drier, and he understood that the drawing had to be beaten on one side in order to be embossed on the other, and that it wasn't necessary to erase the pencil line because from the other side it couldn't be seen. Thanks, he said, and asked himself to whom he had said thanks. To thee, he answered. He had a strange sensation, a trembling: as if it were not he who was constructing something but rather something that was constructing him, and getting to his feet, he felt humble, like a worthless gift. He took the copper, lay it on the block, drew a deep breath, and began again to tap the chisel along the outline he had drawn: this caused the spike to stand out better still and to mature, the way he wanted. He felt the wood resound under his blows, and make the floor shake, which in turn made his own feet shake; thus the blows came from him and returned to him, as if he were fashioning himself. He had a little burlap bag brought to him and had it filled with dry sand. He packed it as full as he could and tied it shut with a leather thong. He took a new sheet of copper and heated it in the fire: you could see it getting hot because it was turning white. Finally it had the whiteness of the sun behind a mist, that was the sign it was soft. He withdrew it. In the air it cooled rapidly and darkened, covering over with oxidation. He plunged it into the urine. The copper sputtered, sent up steam. The crust came loose and floated around on the surface. The urine was green. He took the copper out of the liquid and held it straight in front of him, wondering what to make with it: a dove, a cluster of grapes, an ox and a donkey, a saint, a loaf of bread? Bread is something we almost never eat, only when we can afford to. Bread wasn't right. We have never had donkeys, they're used in the mountains. An ox and a donkey signify a birth, the altar signifies the opposite. It was better to draw grapes, with the spike of wheat you make bread, with the grape you make wine; whereas if you draw an already made loaf, on the other side you'd have to put already made wine, and that means a glass. It would be wisest to draw the new grape, like the one the saint of the altar used to eat at the noon-time and evening meals: she would walk under the arbors, detach some bunches, clean the fruit with two fingers to get rid of the sulfate dusting, then one by one put them into her mouth. Animals would gather around her, for when one eats, all can eat; and they who eat alone, die alone. She would toss some grapes on the ground, they would roll about, the poultry would chase after them with wide-open beaks. Once she found a hedgehog under the leaves. She didn't know whether it would eat grapes, but anyhow she put a few in front of its snout and watched. The hedgehog was sleeping in the dewy grass, the odor of the grapes woke it and put it on its guard: it curled up into its defense position, its nose tucked under its belly. She bent down to pick up the grapes, so they'd not be spoiled. Bending, she emitted a sigh. She was

fond of grapes. One may draw grapes. There's nothing else one may draw.

At that moment he heard the bells sounding noon.
One of the children came to tell him that the meal was
ready. He felt desperate: the whole morning had
gone into engraving one spike, he would be unable to
do anything else. He was not worthy of the saintly
one: he had but this single opportunity to become
worthy of her, and he was in the midst of losing it,
partly because of what was wrong with his leg, partly
because of what was wrong with his hands, partly
because of his fever. He looked at his hands: they
were a bit swollen, the blood was not circulating
properly. There was a weight in his head, like an
undissolved clot: fever. Anyhow, it was possible to
keep going, a lot more than that can be put up with.
He was afraid of wanting to vomit when he ate; also
out of respect for others, he had his plate brought to
him in the workshop, and sat down on a tool chest.
As he chewed, he considered the sheet of copper; it
wasn't very wide, the bunch of grapes would have to
be vertical, long and narrow, with five clusters of
fruit, two side by side above, two side by side below,
plus another underneath; but above the cluster you
could draw a branch with a shoot on the left and a
tendril on the right; the tendril had to be done like the
tail of a pig. The idea was good, he didn't want it to
get away from him. He put his plate on the floor and
returned to work; with the pencil he drew the figure

he had in his head. If someone walked by and saw the untouched plate, he'd think he hadn't eaten because of the fever and would call the doctor; goodbye altar. He glanced at the plate: it was bare and gleaming, someone had eaten everything, licked it clean—that made a good impression. With a little thought you could figure out whether it had been a cat or a rooster, but he didn't have the time. He drew the cluster of grapes and what came out best was the tendril, to him it had an original and joyous look, full of mischief. Gaity made him hungry. Today was Friday; he would eat on Monday, after the procession. The hardest drawing to get right was that of the grapes themselves. Each came out different from the others, when in reality they are all the same, round and fat. An idea came to him; he found a hollow iron tube about the thickness of his little finger, he sawed off a length of it and filed it thin at one end. He tested it at once: he placed the tapered end directly over one of the grapes he had drawn and tapped with the hammer on its other end: the grape came out perfect, as round as could be, and it was embossed on the other side. He made all the others the same way. Looking at the just completed cluster, he felt such satisfaction that he thought for a moment that he could construct altars for the rest of his days. This thought delighted him at first, then left him downcast when it led to the idea that someone else could very well construct a similar altar using his chisels. He decided that, the work once finished, he would destroy the tools, or have them buried with him in his grave. For the present they were working, and even though it wasn't necessary, since he had finished chiseling the figure, he took care to touch up the point of each chisel with a file, fearing it had been dulled in the course of the work. The cluster behind him, he engraved the branch, and above the branch a leaf. He now had the wheat for the making of the Host—thou must write it with a capital—, the wheat to sheathe the left leg of the altar; and he had the grapes for making the wine which filled the chalice, to sheathe the right leg of the altar. He would build the altar out of wood, but he would leave the top as is, in pure wood, because it is always covered by a white cloth, and upon the cloth goes the lectern, and upon the lectern, the Gospel; while the legs, due to be visible, would be faced with engraved copper. The work done thus far just barely served to cover one part of the front side of the legs. And there remained only a very small amount of copper, a few thin irregular strips, the scraps. Every time he had undertaken an important piece of work, he had always run short of something. Whatever was lacking inevitably had to be made up for by something else. But this time you couldn't use brass or aluminum or iron. There's plenty of iron around, but it's black and rusts: Mass celebrated on iron resembles Mass celebrated in wartime, a helmeted head saying Mass on an iron altar and several helmeted heads listening to it. When he had heard one of those Masses for the first time, at the front, just to the rear of the trenches, under the shelter of some hills, he had thought it a sacrilege. And in fact, right after the Mass they had distributed special rations, in other words *grappa,* and the soldiers were sent over the top. A blasphemy. No iron altars. It had to be copper. There would have to be a canvass of the village, from house to house, asking them to turn over the copper pots. He called the older children and told them to make the rounds of the big families, where there were two copper pots, and to ask for one of them, carefully explaining why. It was already evening, you could tell from the animals coming home from the fields, and from the field-hands who were moving in groups along the roads. The working day was over, the time for rest was beginning, which, for women, meant taking the kerchief off their heads by untying the knot behind their necks, wrapping an apron around their hips, tying it behind their backs, and thus transformed, setting the table and getting the polenta started. That's where the problem was: it was the moment when copper pots were everywhere in use, and you could hope for a gift of one only in those households where they had two. And now here come the children—one has three pots, another has four, a mountain of copper, enough to build an altar to outdo even St. Peter's. A child comes in with a single pot. This means that he was sent to a street full of misers, but that doesn't matter, thinks my father, what matters is that it was given willingly. He picks it up by the handle, drops it at once: it's hot. Who gave it to you? A family of poor people. Where do they live? Not far away. Why did it take you so long? Because the pot was still on the fire, they were in the middle of making polenta. Then it must be returned to them. But it isn't right to exclude a family from the altar merely because it is poor. My father has an idea: with the tin-snips he cuts a piece of copper out of the poor family's pot, and sets it aside; it will be all right for the altar, all you have to do is insert it in some larger sheet and fasten it with nails. He cuts a somewhat larger piece from a pot belonging to one of the more well to do families and with this he fills the gap left in the poor family's pot, and he fastens it like this: he bores some holes with a little hand-drill, through the holes he slips short copper nails, that is, rivets, he flattens the rivets against the anvil, first on one side and then on the other, to flatten their heads, and thus the patch is tight, leakproof. He orders the pot returned to the family it came from. By now night has fallen, you must go to sleep. He dozes off right there on some blankets.

It's cold, but the fever puts him to sleep, and he dreams. He goes out to hunt in the snow. He sees the footprint of a hare, he counts the marks left by the claws to find out whether it is a hare or a dog—it is a hare. He follows the tracks in order to flush the animal. The way is constantly uphill, you can never see more than a hundred yards ahead, and there's never any end. This hare is not findable. Walking, his feet sink into the snow or perhaps into the earth beneath the snow, the farther he walks, the farther he sinks in, until finally he sinks so far in that his heart beats and beats but does not pump enough blood for him to continue. He presses his hand to his chest, soaked with sweat, and he finds himself awake and dripping, with his hand over his heart. It must be the fever. He gets another blanket and covers himself better. He hears someone snoring in some room and the cows chewing their cud. Reassured, he falls back to sleep. He dreams that a man with three feet—for there exist men with two feet, and men with three feet are men like ourselves except that they look a little like octopuses because the third foot grows from one of their armpits, so that it could even be a third arm, but it extends all the way to the ground—comes to our houses all smiles, and takes a seat while waiting for a friend, after whom he asks. And we all marvel at this friend who must be a man but who has a name ending in the feminine *a*. In any case, he no longer lives among us; he should try to go a little farther up the road, for there has lately been a great deal of moving, it may be that this friend has moved farther, and then, too, he has three legs, those with three legs ordinarily move farther and faster. Disappointed, the man leaves, he proceeds with great difficulty, no one remains in the courtyard, the cattle begin to complain as if they were abandoned, they bellow and bellow and this bellowing wakes everybody up and my father gets up, covered with sweat, and with an ache in his head.

He wakes, and the headache goes away little by little. He looks at the sky through the window panes, it is white; it must be dawn. And it's Saturday. There is no time left to do anything. He gets up in the dark and heads toward the door. He bumps into something and there is a racket that wakes everybody up; the mountain of pots has collapsed, the floor is strewn with supplies of copper. There is also that bit of copper cut from the pot of the poor family, the most precious of all. He will have to draw something on it to put right in front so that everybody sees it. He opens the door and a reddish light floods in, the light of sunrise before the sun appears. He hunts on the ground for the poor family's bit of copper, is unable to find it. He stands up to go and try to let more light in, and sees something in his hand, the bit of copper itself. He discovers that he is gripping it tightly between his fingers, but does not feel it. His fingers are swollen, he is unable to flex them. He touches his knee: swollen. Quite all right. The altar will be an altar. Between the right and the left leg he will put a stretcher, like those in the trestle tables in monasteries, and at the midpoint of this stretcher he will have an escutcheon, and upon this escutcheon he will make a large sculpture, of what he does not yet know. Pending that, he will use the poor family's copper right away, and he has an inspiration. He will pretend that a grape has come loose from the bunch and fallen to the ground, he will draw it on the poor family's piece and will rivet it to the base of the escutcheon, on the side facing the right leg, just under the bunch itself. With this idea he sets straight to work. First he cuts up the pots into pieces, piles the copper sheets beside the hammering block, and begins to hammer. The whole house wakes up, and as each person gets out of bed, he comes down to see what is going on. Then, from daybreak through till the evening, passers-by stop and look in. He who has given a pot has the right to come and see what use is being made of it. Standing up stiff and straight while he works, like a giant, he looks even taller because he is unable to bend his knee, and at all times he has people crouched around him, gazing at him with admiration, then those people go away saying that he won't be able to do it, it would take a month and there is only one day left, it would take so much strength and he hasn't any more: looking at him you see that if he falls, he won't collapse in a heap like a half-empty sack, no, he'll topple, like a felled tree. Even he too senses that he might well end like that, but at least he knows why: as of now he can no longer bend at all, his knee is locked, he must remain erect in order to work. So swollen are his hands that he has trouble grasping the tools; he asks for a basin of cold water, thrusts his hands in up to the wrists; feels that the coolness does him good, that the swelling is abating, that feeling is coming back into his fingers: he tries moving them in the water and they obey him. He takes them out of the basin and holds them in the air, like a surgeon before the operation. He waits for the air to dry them. He flexes the joints. Occasional pauses to rest are helpful, even for thinking. When he finishes preparing the copper that is to cover the feet, we bring him some short thick planks that have been drying for several years. He chooses those best suited for building the altar proper, he raps his knuckles upon them and scratches them with his fingernails, finally settling on elm.

Now begins an easy part of the work, sawing the wood to make the legs of the altar, legs that are to be square, then sawing the wood for the top where the priest will rest the missal, and finally for the stretcher that will connect the legs and upon which is to go the escutcheon that he wants to engrave. This work need not be perfect, for everything will be covered with copper: it is the copper that must be perfect. The wooden structure of the altar is to be built very solidly: a wide, heavy top, two square, pillar-like legs, each resting on a foot whose length matches the width of the top, and a stretcher of the same thickness, with the central escutcheon. They will be able to move it in an ox-cart. He will be on the cart, and will keep a hand on the altar, unnecessary though that will be; but he will do it, not to keep the altar from falling, but to keep from falling himself. He is still working with that fear of keeling over from one minute to the next. Whenever he interrupts his work, he feels his hands trembling (not the fingers but his entire hand, because the swelling has made all his fingers into one) and his legs too (not the knees, because the injured knee no longer bends, but he does find himself bending and flexing his ankle, even when there is no need to). Every hour that passes something else is accomplished, one leg for the altar, another leg, the bolting of the feet, the nailing of the top. And with every hour that passes he raises his eyes and says, I thank thee, and so doing he makes a slight bow: his whole body obeys him as if it had been made solely for bowing. Everything he does is a gift he receives. We do not know what death is. So long as it is not there, it terrorizes us, like every mystery. The mysterious is our enemy. As it gradually reveals itself, our terror fades, light dawns, the mind penetrates that dark space, realizing that it too is visible: death has given way to become but a part of life. He recalls having seen, one summer, a cicada that was singing away: bark-colored against the bark of the branch, it was singing with lowered head as if drunk with happiness, and an inch away from it were the skeletons of its relatives, two empty membranes, dried up, transparent. How good this all is, and how right, he had exclaimed. For an instant he had imagined a generation of cicadas falling mute beside the skeletons of their dead forebears: nature stilled, arid, void. How bad all this is, and how wrong. But what he was in the act of making, the altar, did not belong to the living alone, it belonged above all to the dead: it was a bridge between this world and the next. Death is several things: the silence of a voice, eternal separation, unending distance. The altar is a voice, is a bridge, is a nearness. There are ways to overcome death, every living species has one, from the cicada to mankind. Man has the simplest means: to refrain from killing. He who does not kill, will not die. Death is a choice: it suffices not to choose it. It is an act of will: do not will it, that suffices. A man is stood against a wall, other men shoot at him: those men have chosen death and are in the act of dying, the other will live forever. How clear all that is, and how strange that in order to think about it there need be death. They say that death destroys life; the opposite is true, it preserves it. Life, except for the life of the saints, entails an error: it begins with a birth, and lives in the illusion that birth keeps repeating itself infinitely. Then death comes, and everything turns out to be false, but there is no longer time to correct anything whatever. Only the life that is not blind to death will not be blind to itself. I thank thee, said he, weeping. He had been walking along the path of a life that had begun badly, with a birth, like all lives, and lo, he had stumbled into death, which had always been there, only he had feigned not to see it. Fortunately, this death would never go away again. Up to that moment he hadn't really known what he had been doing: things destined to oblivion. Now he was making an altar. There was no possible comparison between what he was doing now and what he had done hitherto. Not that he had done incorrect things. But with respect to the truth they were inconsistent things: only he who maintains the existence of death present before him proceeds in truth, the others act always with a mental reservation, are afraid of death, and so do not think about it, as though it were not there. The things they do may be beautiful, intelligent, grand. But not true, which is a great deal more. She had let so many occasions go by for making herself remembered. But when she was alive, no one thought about it. Now those occasions were re-emerging, were being sought out and clad in copper that they might last forever. When she was alive it was as if she hadn't been: everyone had gone about living within his own life. Now that she was dead, we strove by every means to hold on to her. When she was alive, few people knew she existed. Now many knew, the altar would be a reminder of it forever and for everybody. How simple all that was, and how easy, and how painless. Had she not fooled the men who were pursuing the stranger, had the stranger been killed, and had she not been taken away, how sad all that would be. Had he not injected that water into his knee, had he fired upon the enemy and had healthy legs now, how unbearably painful all this would be. Had each of them lived as society wishes, what a shameful life would they have had. Christ is, and there is none other like unto Him. If He were not, to live would be an insipid folly. How horrible that must be, to be a soldier, to be a clerk, to be a citizen conforming to the rules. You would have thought that someone of extraordinary intelligence and worldly power had perfectly understood what is right, and then had ordained the doing and the having done of just the opposite. It is false, our way of being born, of baptizing, of marrying, of working, of having a child, of going to the hospital, of making war, of dying; it is rendered false by the error of deceit. When we baptize a child and when we marry, our immediate concern is how to notify the relatives and friends, which relatives and which friends, and who to invite to the feast and who not; as if every event in life were a weapon or an occasion for taking a long-awaited revenge. It is likewise as regards career, money, power.

The one, the definitive exception is death: that death which enters your house, prevents you from steering life, from directing it against whomever you like, forces you to halt. If death has entered your house, your enemy also can walk in, sure to suffer no offense. There's something strange about this idea, something not clear. It's as if . . . as if the real truth were the exact opposite of the apparent truth. We believe that death is murder and strife. Instead death is a truce in the bloody struggle that is life: during that truce each may look around him and finally understand. How clear everything became when the cries of the enemy soldier who was dying only a few feet from him subsided and became a death-rattle. Can't they take him somewhere else. He can't get up out of his fox-hole. Throw him something, then, medicine, morphine. Can't see where he is, can't wave to him. Well, let's do something, anything. Can't talk about him; he's in the middle of dying, let him die. And here is the solution, clear, valid for everybody: you take the syringe you didn't realize until then that you had on you, you fill it with putrid water, it's all over the place, you uncover a knee, hold it in such a way that it's relaxed, feel for the tendons and the kneecap with a finger, you don't feel anything because your hands are cold; so you warm them up, putting them in front of your mouth and blowing on them, you feel again for the tendons so as to get the steel needle past without cutting them, if a man weren't dying a few feet away you would go on hesitating forever; instead you are very calm and so determined you are amazed at yourself, you drive the point of the needle a little way, but only a little way, under the skin, the skin doesn't bleed because it's cold and the blood doesn't flow, so you drive it in a little more and hold it there to get accustomed to the pain; the dying man has even brought his death-rattle down, now it is barely breath, you'd think he is in a hurry, and so you drive the needle a little farther in, again a twinge of pain like the one before, but not worse, therefore bearable, simply get used to it, the one who is dying draws another breath, he seems to breathe only when the needle's progress stops, as if to say there is no time for pauses, then with your left hand you pull the kneecap upward so that it doesn't get in the way of the steel point that is going in, then with the right hand you give another push to the needle which, thus unobstructed, penetrates, goes in beside the kneecap, passes beyond the latter, avoids the bone, and its hollow point lands in the middle of a skein of little nerves; now you have only to press it very gently, almost to guide it between one nerve and the other, then stop it amidst these delicate filaments, and unload the poisonous fluid. The syringe is big, not all the fluid comes out, there isn't enough room. You wait a bit. Then press the plunger again, all the way to the bottom. The fluid forms a large lump, as though instead of water you had injected a ball. You take the syringe out and throw it away, it will never be used again. With your hand you massage the swollen lump, so as to spread the fluid everywhere, inflaming the veins as well as the nerves. It's done. While you continue to soothe your faintly trembling knee with your right hand, you become aware that something is missing from the world. You listen and you understand: the dying man wails no more.

Now you are here, hand upon your swollen, faintly trembling knee, and you look at the altar, barely built; it is dark, it may already be morning; the wooden part is finished, cut and put together, the copper sheathing is still in separate sheets, they have to be smelted and joined and there's still no drawing for the escutcheon. Several days would be needed; he has only a few hours.

19

Of what happened after that we members of the family have only a sketchy understanding. We remained awake in the rooms upstairs, respecting his wish to build the altar unaided. We heard him stirring about, banging, hammering, even breathing. Every so often, silence; and in that silence we heard the crackling of the fire, which meant he was heating copper, getting ready to engrave it. Suddenly we hear a distinct thud: we go downstairs and find him stretched full length on the floor. With his hands he is trying to reach some tin-snips, also on the ground and lying a few inches away from his fingertips. He is kicking his feet, struggling in vain to find something

to brace himself against so that he can push himself
forward. We lift him and carry him to his bed. He
protests that this way he is lost, he'll have no time
left. We try to calm him. People passing along the
street at this late hour stop, seeing the fire burning at
the front of the forge, and want to know who is
working so late, or so early, for it is not yet dawn. The
house fills up with people, some of them we don't
even know. The presence of so many persons after
two days of solitude bewilders him and quiets him
down: he lets himself be put to bed, he lets himself be
covered and tucked in, he says thank you, he feels he
has a fever, he says he is going to die. He gives his
hand to strangers, enjoins everyone not to touch his
tools, not to take the copper away, not to put the fire
out. He says that he feels sick for the first time, or
sicker than all the other times, that he has never been
so sick, and that he will die: but he wants to die with
the job going forward, it mustn't be abandoned.
Everyone agrees, that's the way it should be, he has
done more than he possibly could. They swear to him
that everything will be left as is, the copper, the tools,
the altar, the fire. He falls asleep.

Three hours later we see bright red light filtering
through the cracks in the balcony. It must be sunrise.
The light grows and is making a noise. We go to the
window. Father, Son, and Holy Ghost. The house is
burning. The fire had got to the door of the workshop,
entered, reached the floor boards overhead and the
balcony. My father is sleeping in the middle of

flames, he seems dead. My brother leaps onto the joists, grabs my father under the arms, hauls him out of the room, he leaves him in the storeroom and runs to get a hatchet. Women are climbing ladders with buckets of water, my brother chops at the burning floor boards, the bed falls through to the floor below, sparks flying. Down there the children are spraying everything with the copper sulfate pump. The fire is fought through the windows and from the lower floor; but the wooden altar is in danger of catching. My father lets out a shout that startles us, because no one recognizes his voice, and there's the altar moving slowly toward a corner, it's my father pulling it with a rope wound round his waist and over his shoulder, my brother's children have the spray directed at him so he won't get burned. Soon the flames die down even in the workshop, where there is no more door or ceiling, but where the walls and floor are covered with water, and the fire goes out. Father, Son, and Holy Ghost. With painful efforts my father attempts to rekindle it in front of the door that has vanished, he gathers branches and dried twigs, makes them into a pile, ignites it with paper and gasoline. That's what he needs to smelt the copper and get on with his work. We try to persuade him to stop, we try to pull him away, but he shakes himself loose. He doesn't even listen to us. He slept three hours, he has got just enough strength back to push on with his work for another half-day. My sister-in-law is the best-hearted and most thoughtful woman in the world; if anyone needs help anywhere in the world, she is ready to drop everything and go to his aid. She had slept at the foot of my father's bed, to be there while he rested if there were anything he needed; now she sees him in this state, sopping wet, with his clothes half burned away, and she talks to him with a smile still on her face although tears are beginning to well from her eyes. She pretends it's nothing—all our faces are wet with the water that had been thrown around and sprayed—but when the tears gather in rivulets, she goes off to cry undisturbed. There is a great silence now, broken only by my father's hammer-blows as he begins to fashion the central escutcheon, the large round shield that will adorn the stretcher connecting the two legs of the altar. He joins together five sheets of copper by superimposing and bending the edges as you do with sheets of paper. He cuts this large sheet into a circular shape. He turns its edge, hammers it flat. The result is a circle composed of five vertical, interlocked panels, the longest one in the center, the others tapering off in length on each side. He wonders what to draw. On the day of her burial a flock of sheep passed by, perhaps coming from the Abruzzi. Those shepherds turn up once a year and scatter their sheep around in the fields where they graze on the stubble. Once he went hunting and he is walking through the fields wearing his cloak and with his double-barrelled shotgun slung muzzle down, you can see the two barrels sticking below the hem of the cloak. He comes upon a shepherd standing at the edge of a field; the sheep raise and lower their heads out of habit, but there is nothing on the ground they can get their teeth into. He goes up to the shepherd and points off toward a field where the sheep will be able to find something to eat. The shepherd was suspicious, afraid of being fooled by someone whose only wish was to get rid of him. Then he sees the barrels of the shotgun and very quickly asks, "Yes? Another field? Where?" and without waiting for an answer, whistles to his dogs and with bites and shoves his poor sheep are driven off toward other horizons. My father was disappointed, perhaps he ought to have concealed the shotgun; and that scene of a shepherd he had frightened away remained forever in his mind. Now there is something he can do to remedy it: he will make a shepherd standing motionless in the center panel, and this one will never go away from us. He draws him. He is uncertain whether to give him trousers. Usually they are drawn wearing a tunic. But the ones from the Abruzzi never wear tunics. He draws a poor man with trousers and a sheepskin vest, stooped because he comes from the Abruzzi and with an eye that looks sidewise to see whether someone is about to chase him away. No one will ever chase him again. On each of the other panels he draws a sheep, all of them turned toward the shepherd. The two nearer ones have their heads lifted, the two farther away are grazing. There's no dog.

20

The procession arrives at ten, the singing and the treading of feet are heard, there is no altar, the memorial is empty. The priest enters and blesses the air, the walls, the floor. Now this place is consecrated. From the crossroads they hear the sound of a hammer. It's my father, still working, although it no longer has any point. There is a road in madness that must be followed to its end, because to stop is more dangerous than to continue.

The whole altar is finished at noon, two hours late. It is taken to the now deserted crossroads in a cart, in the cart my father stands, one hand placed on the

117

altar but not to keep it steady, only to keep himself from falling. The cart drawn by oxen advances slowly. It halts in front of the memorial. The altar is unloaded and moved inside, placed squarely in the center of the sanctified space, turned toward the door and the bells. My father raps his knuckles on the wood, then sinks down in a corner. He has his holiday clothes on. He prays in a whisper.

The procession disperses off in the countryside, people in small groups head back toward their homes. They see the altar that was not there before and shake their heads: everybody knew it wasn't going to be ready in time.

The last to arrive is the priest, he sees the altar and stops. He enters with the missal in his hand. He touches the altar, runs his hands over it from one end to the other. He looks at the copper figures which seem in even higher relief in the contrasting sunlight and shadow. He thinks about them in turn. He is leaving when he overhears a groan. He turns and sees my father. "Are you the one who did this?" he asks. My father nods, acquiescing, then extends his arms to say that it has been to no purpose. The priest hesitates, as though what he is about to do were too much. Then he turns slowly so as to be able to see the church through the window, places the opened missal on the altar, touches the altar with both his hands; he signs himself, stands with open palms, bows his head and kisses the altar and remains thus bowed over it for a long time, his forehead upon the wooden surface. Then he slowly straightens, saying:

"In nomine Patris"—he makes a broad sign of the cross—, *"et Filii, et Spiritus Sancti. Amen."*

My father gets up by supporting himself against the wall, scraping against the brick, when he gains his feet he too makes the sign of the cross. He stands straddle-legged so as not to fall.

The priest extends his arms to right and left, his hands open, palms forward. In a strong voice he says:

"Veni, sanctificator, omnipotens aeterne Deus, et bene"—he repeats the sign of the cross, lowers his hands upon the table—*"dic hoc altare, tuo sancto nomini dedicatum."*

My father is holding himself erect by clinging to the wall itself, he seeks something to take a grip upon, he is about to fall.

The priest prays in a low voice, then concludes:

"Ut meum ac vestrum sacrificium acceptabile fiat apud Deum Patrem omnipotentem."

He joins his hands palm against palm in prayer, and says:

"Domine, exaudi orationem meam."

He bows his head. He waits. It is for my father to continue. My father hasn't the strength, he is scarcely able to keep upright. But he moves his lips and in a voice barely audible,

"Clamor meus," he murmurs, *"ad te veniat."*

21

Thus built and inaugurated, the altar remained in the monument for months and was completely useless. But it was to have a glorious destiny, for our village church (a thirteenth century convent with Byzantine-Gothic frescoes in the cupola above the apse) owing to the reform that was about to go into effect, had no new altar from which the priest would be able to say Mass facing his flock. To this end a platform had been prepared. All the parishioners, however, were eager to have the platform replaced by a more worthy altar, but the village could not afford such a luxury.

And then one morning a little party of parishioners

arrived, sent to my father with a request: would he be willing to see the altar he had made become the altar used for regular Mass? No one had ever thought of that. It exceded all our hopes.

In order to answer this hallowed purpose, in order to receive the sanctified stone, the altar was modified. In the center of the top a space was let in, a square some eight inches on a side and two deep. Into this hollow was inserted and sealed a stone of the same dimensions. It contained some bones of a man, born in Venice, who, five hundred years before, had fought against the Germans. He had been taken prisoner and in prison had made a vow to dedicate himself to good works if he was freed; he was freed and founded an organization called "The Company of the Poor" with the mission of taking in, assisting, and educating orphans, and because of the experience he gained thereby he was asked to come to Padua, Vicenza, Brescia, Bergamo, Pavia, Milan to teach the bishops and leaders of those cities how to establish or reorganize charitable institutions which excluded the asking of alms and were based upon productive work and education, with a severe distinction drawn between the spiritual and the temporal: to any and all the door would be open, with no votive offering required.

This man contracted the plague while visiting the sick. The viaticum was administered to him with great solemnity, and summoning all the ecclesiastics of his house he had them swear that even though he were a layman, or a protestant (Luther had founded his religion some decades before) no one would ever be barred from "The Company of the Poor," provided he were indeed poor and sought admission.

His body is entombed in the oratorio of San Bartolomeo at Somasca in the province of Bergamo. Beatified by Benedict XIV, canonized by Clement XIII, proclaimed Universal Patron of Orphans by Pius XI, an altar with relics was raised to him at Venice-Mestre by order of John XXIII.

His name is of no importance. Every altar has its Sacred Stone and upon this stone is placed the Gospel for the reading and the chalice for the consecration. Every Sacred Stone contains relics. In this way all altars are linked together, and all Masses are celebrated over the bones of martyrs: this realizes in fact what the Church calls "The Communion of Saints." To name the one who happens to be closest to my mother has no meaning, because this is an unbroken chain which begins before Christ and will endure throughout the ages to come.

At the moment when the Sacred Stone was fitted into its place I imagined my mother standing aside to make room for her new friend.

Being done testifying unto her transformation into an altar, only made possible by the love, the culture, and the piety characteristic of her world, whence I come, I feel that in writing this book I have done exactly the same thing, building to her this altar of words, according to the love, the culture, and the piety of the world whence I am an emigrant.

The design of this book is the work of Marjorie Merena, of Brattleboro, Vermont. The typesetting has been by American-Stratford Graphic Services, Inc., also of Brattleboro, Vermont. It has been printed by McNaughton & Gunn, Inc., Ann Arbor, Michigan.